LASHES OF LIGHTNING

(A SATIRICAL STORY OF FREE RADICALS)

ANOOP CHANDOLA

iUniverse®

LASHES OF LIGHTNING
(A SATIRICAL STORY OF FREE RADICALS)

iUniverse books may be ordered through booksellers or by contacting:

iUniverse
1663 Liberty Drive
Bloomington, IN 47403
www.iuniverse.com
844-349-9409

ISBN: 978-1-6632-2502-3 (sc)
ISBN: 978-1-6632-2501-6 (hc)
ISBN: 978-1-6632-2500-9 (e)

Library of Congress Control Number: 2021915063

Print information available on the last page.

iUniverse rev. date: 07/27/2021

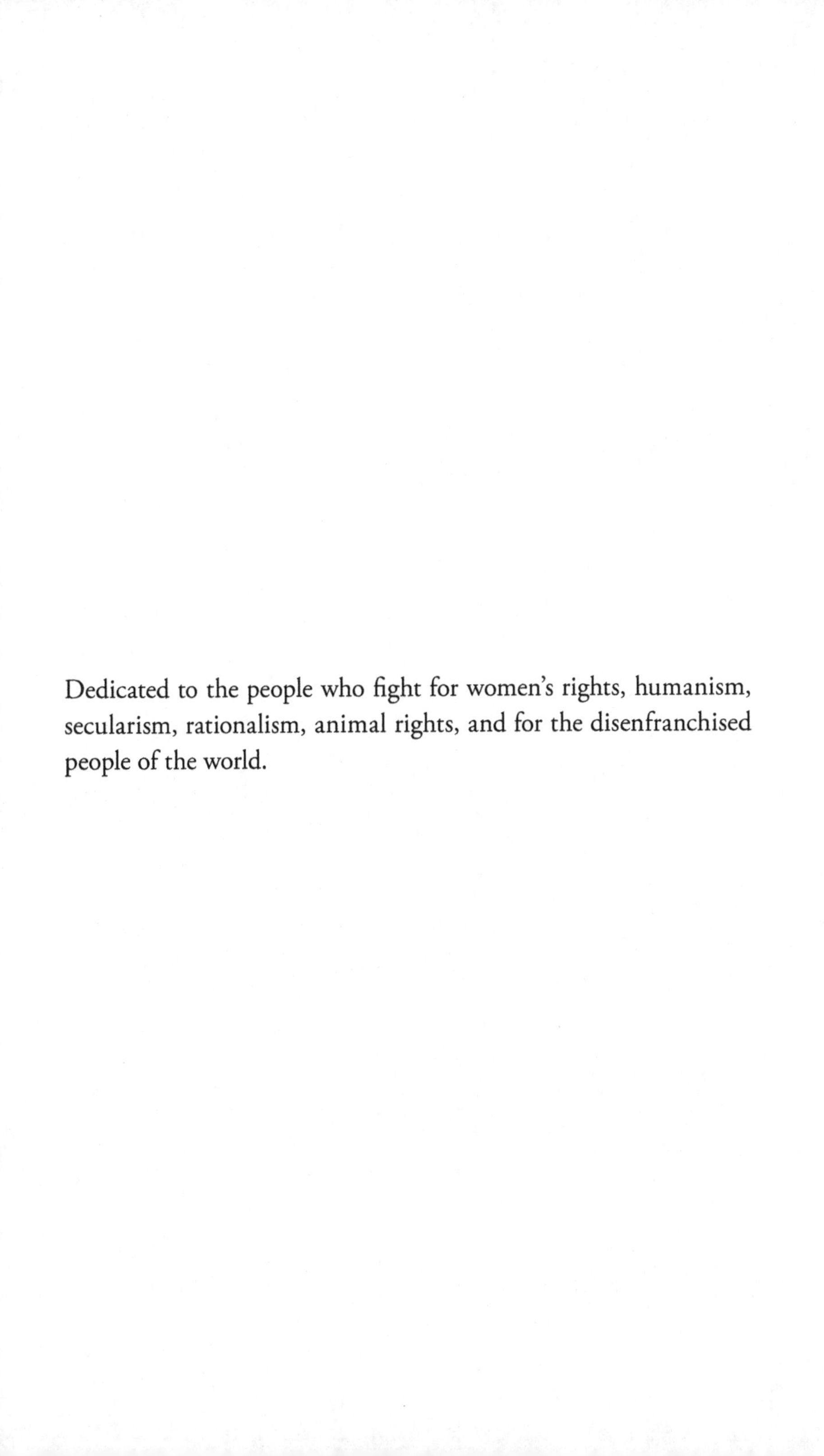

Dedicated to the people who fight for women's rights, humanism, secularism, rationalism, animal rights, and for the disenfranchised people of the world.

ACKNOWLEDGEMENTS

I AM GRATEFUL to my publisher's team. Thanks to my wife Sudha and my son Varn for their help. I don't have enough words to thank my sister-in-law, Professor Tashi Pant, for her help proofreading my earlier work.

CHAPTER ONE

BIJLI VIVIDLY REMEMBERS the last day of the Spring Flower Festival the year she turned eight. Like the other young girls of the village, she regularly participated in the Central Himalayan festival, which began on the first day of spring. Every day of spring, the girls collected wild Himalayan flowers and dropped them the next morning at the doorstep of every house. On the morning of the last day of the festival, householders would drop token cash into every girl's flower basket, welcoming the first day of summer and hoping for much-needed warmth in the cold Himalayan mountains.

To celebrate the last day of the festival, Bijli had collected flowers from her garden—all fruit and vegetable flowers—with the help of her father's gardener. Instead of one basket, she had two baskets full of flowers—one for the festival and one to celebrate her mother's safe return from the pilgrimage to the four holy places in the Garhwal Himalayas, the roof of the world. She had thought her father would be happy to see her mother, Sarsuti, safely return from the treacherous pilgrimage: high mountains, raging rivers, heavy snowfall, dense wild forests, tigers and bears, and, of course, high altitude sickness and fatigue. Nevertheless, devout pilgrims are not discouraged by these difficulties; they would travel from here to Tibet without breaking a sweat in order to view the holy mountain of Kailash standing tall and snow-clad. It is believed that this mountain was the abode of Lord Shiva and his wife Parvati, the Mountain Goddess.

Sarsuti did return safely, but she was late by two days because the road had been damaged in a landslide. As soon as she stepped inside her room, she saw Shyamal Kandyal, her husband and Bijli's father, waiting for her with a bamboo whip in his hand. Shyamal was a government contractor employed to build a portion of about 20 miles of the first road stretching between the small towns of Pauri and Srinagar. The British rulers of India planned to eventually connect India with Tibet by this road. Shyamal, heavily built and over six feet tall, was tough with his workers. He never hesitated to whip a worker he found resting from his work to smoke.

Sarsuti was Shyamal's third wife, and she shared the house with his two senior wives. He used to beat Sarsuti as he considered her, unlike the two senior wives, whom he never beat, lazy. Sarsuti had only one child, Bijli. The senior wives were fortunate: the first wife had two daughters and a son and the second wife had four daughters and a son. Shyamal might have spared Sarsuti if she too had given him a son. He earned sufficient money to maintain his large polygamous family under one roof. On Sundays he would ride his white horse and go hunting with his rifle. No wife accompanied him on his hunts, thus giving him an opportunity to cheat on them.

After all, how was a polygamous husband expected to remain faithful?

Shyamal was quite vigilant about his wives, however. His polygamous cousin's fourth wife was found to be secretly involved in a relationship with a man of her age, an untouchable. Inter-caste marriage was prohibited in Hinduism. Indeed, scriptures like the *Bhagavad Gita* forbade inter-caste marriages and their progeny. Like most Hindus, Shyamal was a devotee of the Lord of the *Bhagavad Gita*, his devotion evident from the pictures of Krishna hanging in his living room. Two of the largest pictures were his favorites. One of them had Krishna in the middle, dancing with his cowherd *gopi* girlfriends, including Radha, another *gopi* who was married to another man. The other had Krishna eating with his eight wives. According to Hindu mythology, all eight wives were equally devoted to Lord Krishna. There are several myths about how Krishna, an avatar of God, was married to these extraordinarily beautiful women.

Bijli ran to her mother's room when she heard her screams. No neighbor came to rescue Sarsuti, as wife-beating was considered a private matter. Bijli stood stupefied as Shyamal shouted at Sarsuti, calling her *randi,* 'whore.' "You *randi* came so late from your pilgrimage! It was your duty to collect the cow dung and carry it to the basmati fields!"

Each household in this small village had barns with farm animals—cows, oxen, and buffalo—not to mention several men and women. The barns had to be free from dung every day. Two households had goats and sheep, too; unlike other farm animals, they were raised for meat. Bijli and her mother were the only villagers who did not eat meat.

Sarsuti didn't dare raise her hand to stop her husband. Her tall figure—seven inches over five feet—was nevertheless weak compared to her muscular husband. Moreover, in this culture a husband is called "Malik" (Master)!

"Baba, don't beat Ma," Bijli pleaded. Shyamal slapped her. "No, Baba! No, Baba!" She stretched out her hands to stop his slaps. He beat Sarsuti until she fell down because her legs hurt. Somehow, she got up and limped out to the front yard, Bijli following her.

The following morning, on the last day of the spring festival, some neighbors saw Sarsuti collecting cow dung. A woman, the only literate woman in the entire village, asked her why she was limping. Ironically, Sarsuti was not literate even though she was named after Sarasvati, the goddess of learning. Sarsuti is in fact the colloquial Garhwali pronunciation of Sarasvati. She managed a smile. "I fell down while returning from my pilgrimage." The woman was not fooled by her smile, though.

Bijli decided not to participate in the festival. She dumped her flowers in the heap of cow dung while helping her mother. The woman was surprised and asked her why she didn't join the other girls. "My father beat my mother. I want to help her carry cow dung," she said and burst into tears.

The woman, Chaiti, understood and said, "I will help you." Later she wrote a letter to Gunanand, Sarsuti's brother.

Gunanand understood his sister's plight and thought of dealing with Shyamal, a sex-maniac, polygamist, and bully. It was a dilemma for him. Why did his monogamous parents, who always respected each other even when they had the occasional disagreement, give away his sister to a polygamist? But some of his monogamous relatives had very unhappy married lives, thought Gunanand, monogamy only exacerbating the problems in their lives because there was no divorce and separation was merely acceptable. Why didn't his parents investigate Shyamal's ancestry? Shyamal was not the first polygamist in his ancestry or in the world. Gunanand thought his parents naïve.

For a few minutes he ruminated with anguish while holding that letter in his hand, and in the end he decided to act boldly rather than just talking to his brother-in-law.

In about two months, he returned from America. Instead of going to his village of Dangchaura in Tehri Garhwal, he arrived at Bijli's village of Kandi. It was pitch dark. He wanted to surprise Sarsuti after Chaiti had written to him about her plight.

The following morning, nobody could find Bijli and Sarsuti anywhere. Gunanand had taken them away to his village of Dangchaura. He advised Sarsuti never to return to Kandi. Bijli, however, wanted to go back to her village and be with her girlfriends. Gunanand offered her a better deal, which she accepted. She went to San Francisco with her engineer uncle Gunanand. He had graduated from the University of California at Berkeley and was now working in a small company working on incipient computer technology. Like many other graduates from this university, he became a radical and an atheist. In fact, he never believed the claims of the *Bhagavad Gita,* that Lord Krishna created the universe, but then the Brahmin authors of the *Gita* never anticipated the enlightening power of science and technology!

CHAPTER TWO

BIJLI WAS DEVASTATED when her Uncle Gunanand was hit by a drunk driver while crossing the street. He had been rushed to the ER, but before Bijli reached the hospital, he was already dead. She honored his wish and requested the hospital donate his body to the nearest medical college. No cremation! Gunanand didn't believe in rites and rituals.

One day she found a manuscript on his bookshelf, his memoirs, some short and some long. Some she found to be strange, and she wanted to share them with her two girlfriends, students at Berkeley. Later, both adopted Indian names. Maya, a black woman, was an undergraduate majoring in South Asian studies, and Indira, a white woman, majored in Anthropology.

Maya learned Sanskrit from Professor Murray Emeneau, whose linguistic work in Dravidian languages made him a famous Indologist. Indira, on the other hand, was influenced by Professor John Gumperz, who developed a new interdisciplinary field combining linguistics, sociology, and anthropology called "discourse analysis."

Their academic interests made the three girls close, but their shared atheism brought them even closer. Maya and Indira had their reasons to become non-believers. The stories of two of their girlfriends were the reasons.

One of the women's brother was molested by her church's priest, after which her entire family abandoned the church. If there had been a God, her brother would have been saved by Him.

The other woman's father was a member of an American missionary organization engaged in converting the natives of a South American tribe. The chief of the tribe was happy to see the translation of the Bible in his native language, but some tribal members, including the chief, still had difficulty reciting the Lord's prayer. They were not happy even when they were given money to accept Christianity. One night the lodge where the missionary was staying caught fire and three members died. Her father somehow survived, and that night he understood the falsity of the Lord's prayer. He began to defend the culture of the natives. He even told the chief that there was no God. If He existed, then He would have ended American slavery in two seconds, not in two hundred years.

Bijli, Maya, and Indira often met at the university cafeteria for lunch. Bijli would narrate her uncle Gunanand's memoirs to them, not in any chronological order. The name Gunanand was made of two Hindi words—*gun* means "virtue" and *anand* means "joy." It was quite a common name in the Garhwal Himalayas, where it was often misspelled as Guna Nand. Maya and Indira jokingly called the memoirs *Gun Gossips*. Soon, both the girls began to realize that the memoirs consisted of socially explosive experiences, as were the views of Gunanand.

CHAPTER THREE

THE MEMOIR RELATED to Ali was the one that Bijli started with.

After two years at Berkeley, Gunanand's Indian Muslim friend, Ali, had invited him to his wedding to a beautiful white American girl. He was surprised because Ali had been a shy Indian, and yet he had the courage to execute his "love marriage" plan at Berkeley. Ali's parents had hoped he would marry his uncle's daughter, and he was sure his parents would want her to wear a burqa in the presence of adult males. He promised he would marry her after he returned from America, but when he met Melinda at Berkeley, everything changed radically. Even his diet, which now included pork and wine, both prohibited in Islam.

On the day of their wedding, Ali and Melinda went to the court in the morning and were married legally by a judge. No Muslim or Christian ceremonies. Gunanand liked their liberal beliefs. They had a mixed buffet, vegetarian and non-vegetarian. In the evening, about a dozen of Ali's friends gathered in a restaurant, which had a good-sized dining area reserved for Ali's party. In Ali's home town of Allahabad, there would have been a huge gathering of people, including scores of relatives and friends of the bride and the bridegroom and their parents, not to mention the musicians, sweepers, beggars, etc.

Melinda and Ali held each other's hands and danced before the dinner. Other friends joined them, but not Gunanand. He was approached by a beautiful girl who saw him sitting alone at a corner table. He thought she would ask him for a dance. Instead, she asked him, "May I sit with you?"

Gunanand stood up, smiled, and extended a chair to her. Both sat down and introduced themselves.

"I am Tamara, a classmate of Melinda."

"And I am Gunanand, Ali's classmate from India."

"Yes, Ali told me already. He told me that you are a vegetarian and don't drink. I don't drink either, but I am not a vegetarian. I would very much like to be, though. So, tell me. What vegetarian dishes would you recommend?"

"Before I give you a list of the best Indian vegetarian dishes, may I ask you the reason for you being a teetotaler, if you don't mind?"

"Sure. My father was a raging alcoholic, and he died of cirrhosis at the age of fifty-two. My mother could not control his drinking, but she made sure I never picked up the habit."

"Ah, your mother seems like my mother. The day I was about to leave my Himalayan home, she cried, 'Promise that you will not drink or smoke.' I understood that it was because of my father, who smoked cigarettes and loved to drink whisky. He was not like that before he joined the British Indian Army during World War II. He befriended his English commander, who was popular among the Indian soldiers because he treated them with respect, which meant including them in his whisky-drinking and cigarette-smoking sessions."

Tamara laughed.

Gunanand continued, "A few years after the war, my father received news that the commander had been admitted to a hospital in London. He was battling cancer. The doctors could not save his life."

"You will live much longer since you follow a vegetarian diet."

"Health isn't the reason I am a vegetarian. The reasons are cultural."

"What culture?"

"The culture of non-violence. In my Himalayan culture, people love to eat meat. Wild animals such as deer, quail, boar, and wild pigeons are hunted for meat. In my hometown, the meat of goats and sheep is quite popular. I used to see their skinned bodies hanging on the wall. The butcher would cut any piece the customer liked. Most customers were Hindus. Two of the butchers were Muslims—"

"I thought Hindus were vegetarians," Tamara interrupted.

"Lots of Hindus eat meat. At Berkeley I even saw some swamis of the Rama Krishna Mission eating meat. The Bengali swamis of the Mission loved to eat fish, and the Bengali founder swami of the Mission ate beef once, knowingly. Can a swami become a leader of Hinduism even if he eats beef one time only, and deliberately? Ironically, his vegetarian guru was proud of him! His name was Rama Krishna, but his favorite deity was *Devī* or *Kālī*, a meat-eating goddess, a buffalo-beef-eating goddess. Other swamis of the Mission were strict vegetarians. In Hinduism every swami is expected to observe the vow of *ahimsa*. Mahatma Gandhi was not a swami, but he observed that ancient vow as advocated by Jainism and Buddhism—and by Yoga too. Gandhi detested those political leaders who promoted violence to achieve their ends. No violent person can be a leader without the support of a violent group. Gandhi's example were the violent Nazis, the big lie-followers!"

"Pardon me, but what is the ancient vow you just mentioned?"

"You mean *ahimsa*?"

"Yes."

"It means non-killing. No killing of any animal for food. But let me add that an average meat-eating Hindu does not eat meat regularly."

"You mean an average Hindu eats vegetarian meals most of the time?"

"Right. Meat is costly in India. My parents, like other Himalayan natives, enjoyed meat whenever it was available, but they knew that those dead animals' bodies hanging in the butcher shops drove me toward non-violence in terms of diet. We have no right to kill any living being."

"I agree with you. You have changed my naïve classification of dietary choice. Some like to be vegetarian, and some don't. I understand animal cruelty is a crime. I have a dog. People in some countries eat dog meat. That's animal cruelty."

"Yes, it is. But then dogs are fed with foods that contain the meat of other animals, such as beef."

"I never realized that. You are right; there is animal cruelty for humans and animal cruelty for other animals too."

"But if a deer falls from a cliff and dies, consuming its meat is not animal cruelty. It is just food, non-violent food."

"I understand your point." She softly placed her hand on his hand to show her agreement.

Gunanand felt a sensation.

Later, he often felt that pull and wished to be with her. Whenever he remembered that evening in her company, he would hum Mirza Ghalib's popular Urdu *ghazal*, "*Ye na thī hamārī qismat ki bisāl-e-yār hotā* (This was not in my destiny to have a meeting with my beloved)."

CHAPTER FOUR

"DID YOUR UNCLE use to watch Hindi movies?" Maya asked Bijli.

"Rarely. Among his favorite movies was *Pyāsā*, which means 'thirsty.'"

"Is it a Hindi or Urdu movie?" Indira inquired.

"Call it Hindi or Urdu; it is one and the same language. In the opening credits, the title is written in both Devanagari script as well as Arabic. Because of the use of two scripts, people think Hindi and Urdu are two different languages. But they are not. If you use Roman script instead, nobody would be able to identify whether it is Hindi or Urdu."

"I agree. Professor Gumperz told us that there was a big fuss on All India Radio regarding the question, 'Should Urdu also be used along with Hindi?' An average person has no knowledge of linguistics, the science of language, and from the point of view of linguistics, Hindi and Urdu are two names for one and the same language. Here at Berkeley, the same introductory textbook by Professor John Gumperz and his associates is used teach both Hindi and Urdu. Professor Gumperz was aware of how Indian politicians conveniently evade confessing their ignorance of linguistics by pretending in public that they understand it well," Maya said.

"People should simply use their commonsense or the logic of moviemakers who never studied the topic. The movie title *Pyāsā* is written in Devanagari and Arabic scripts. Doesn't that say something? Indian politicians and nationalists need a mantra: 'Do not politicize knowledge, do not politicize knowledge, do not politicize knowledge,'" Bijli said in support of Maya's point.

"Not all politicians say stupid things, but some do. A minister publicly said that the principle of 'gravitation' was known to ancient Indians, long before Newton stole the concept and elaborated it in his book *Principia*!" Maya laughed as she added, "Ancient India had planes that used the principle of gravitational force, the minister claimed."

"This ignorant minister doesn't realize that he is implying that the Indians were so foolish that they decided to abandon planes in favor of oxcarts to travel long distances!" Bijli quipped.

"Let us come back to your uncle's favorite movie, *Pyāsā*. Why was it his favorite movie?

"That's a long story. I can give you a shorter version, though. As I said, *Pyāsā* means 'thirsty,' and it chokes my throat to even narrate this because of Uncle's personal experience." She took a sip of water and continued. "One late Saturday afternoon, Uncle was in a Bay Area park. He sat on a bench near a huge swimming pool. Beside his bench, a white couple was seated. They were kissing each other. Initially, Uncle ignored them, but when he heard the voice of the woman, he felt he had heard it before. It was Tamara. He never expected to see her again, especially not with a man who was apparently her lover. He mustered the courage and went to her. Upon seeing him, Tamara became momentarily quiet, feigning loss of memory. But the man's facial expression made it clear that he sensed Tamara's pretense. 'How are you, Tamara? I am Gunanand, remember me?' 'Oh, hi,' she responded in a neutral tone. The man intervened and introduced himself to my uncle: 'I am Tamara's husband, Rocky.' The men shook hands. 'Tamara and I met at Ali's wedding reception. Ali was a mutual friend. You are a very lucky husband. Tamara is a brilliant and beautiful lady.'" Bijli laughed as she narrated their discourse.

After a pause, Bijli continued. "Tamara looked embarrassed. She heaved a long sigh and asked, 'How have you been, Gunanand? I never thought I would meet you again!' 'I am very happy to meet you both,' Uncle responded. Rocky could see in their faces the look of long-lost lovers," Bijli said.

"But what has the movie, *Pyāsā,* got to do with your uncle meeting Tamara?" Indira inquired.

"In the movie there is a scene at a party where a poor poet tries to entertain the audience by singing a song. Among the chief guests is the poet's old flame, who is sitting next to her husband. As the poet sings, the old flame cries. Her husband looks unhappy as he sees her tearful eyes gravitating toward the poet, who has his gaze fixed on her," Bijli said as she tried to describe the most dramatic scene of the entire movie.

"What was the song?" Indira inquired.

"Let me translate a couple of lines: *Every companion moves away after giving company for one or two moments. Who has the time to hold the hands of the love-torn people?"*

"Can you sing it?"

"No, I don't have the necessary baritone voice of the singer. Nor can I translate the poetic beauty of the original song, I'm afraid. I have the record and I can play it for you some other time. By the way, the poet presents this song as an Urdu song, but Uncle thought it was an outstanding Hindi song."

CHAPTER FIVE

GUNANAND WASN'T COMFORTABLE seeing Bhanu at the house party arranged by Ruchira and her husband, Ram Jas. The party was meant for a few Indian students of Berkeley—many men and just three women. All of them were unmarried, except one student couple, Preet and his wife Naina.

Bhanu came with his girlfriend, a white girl, who called him Banu. Gunanand knew that Bhanu had not only a wife but also an infant son back in India.

Ruchira had invited Bhanu anyway, but she had no idea that Bhanu would come with his girlfriend, Liz. Nevertheless, she welcomed Liz and introduced her to the other Indians.

Gunanand didn't quite believe Bhanu's story: "My wife wasn't meant for me. She had an affair with a man before we got married. I came to know only after our son was born because her boyfriend came to our home with a gift for the boy."

Before dinner, some of the Punjabi students decided to have a *bhangra* dance. Other non-Punjabis joined them. They clapped and repeated the words *balle balle* loudly.

There was knock on the door. Ram Jas opened the door and found a police officer standing there. "I am sorry to inform you that your neighbor downstairs has complained about excessive noise and kicking the floor."

"Sorry, Officer. I apologize on everyone's behalf. It is just an Indian folk dance. We are Indian students just having a little Indian fun. We will not continue the dance."

"You can continue your dance, but please make sure that it does not cause any nuisance."

Ram Jas was quite impressed with the officer's way of handling the situation. He stopped the dance and proposed music instead. "Anyone who knows Indian music should come forward and sing."

Bhanu stepped forward. All the others surrounded him and sat on the floor. Bhanu started singing, and after a few lines of his *Malkauns raga*, some people in the audience began to whisper.

"Why does he think that he knows singing!"

"Well, some idiots think they have a musical voice and then bore the listeners to death."

Apparently Bhanu noticed them whispering. He even heard a boy whispering, "He should sing only in his bathroom, not in public!" He stopped singing when the whispers changed to whining. The audience gave him polite applause.

"Dinner is ready," Ruchira announced.

It was a vegetarian dinner, and everybody praised her *kari* (curry).

"Bhabhi, your *kari* is exceptional. *Kamāl hai*!" He put his hand over his Sikh turban and saluted her, uttering again in Hindi, "*Ye to kamāl hai* (It's a wonder)."

"Not as good as your Punjabi *kari*. Mine is western U.P. style."

"Bhabhi, give me one more serving. It's so good that, if we were in India, I would have walked barefooted from my hometown of Ludhiana to your hometown of Rampur just for your *kari*."

Ruchira flushed. She brought a big bowl of *kari*. "You made my day, Sohan Bhai."

A few others looked at the bowl. One boy said, "Bhabhi, pass that bowl to us too. No partiality toward Sohan Singh!"

But Liz had a hard time with the hot *kari*. She lost patience, got up and said to Ruchira, "Do you have anything else? This is too spicy for me. I have eaten curry before but not this kind with yogurt and soaked fries, which I don't know what to call."

Ruchira noticed her plight from her panting. She quickly brought her a *rasgulla*. Liz devoured it and stopped panting. "You gave me the right antidote."

"I am sorry for adding too much cayenne powder to those *pakoras*."

"I love this sweet ball. What is it called?"

"This is a famous Bengali sweet. If you ever go to Calcutta, you will find a sweetshop around every corner. People buy a lot of assorted Bengali sweets. I have a friend from Calcutta who is diabetic but can't resist sweets. Her excuse is 'We are all going to die anyway. So why worry and deprive yourself of *rasgulla*!'"

Ruchira laughed with Liz. "You can have some more for dessert, Liz."

CHAPTER SIX

PROFESSOR GUMPERZ AND Professor Emeneau buried Maya under a heap of suggestions before she left for India to do field work.

When she came out of the airport at New Delhi, she was surprised to see not only taxis but also *tangas* (horse carriages). For fun, she decided to take a *tanga*, but on the way to her hotel she had argument with the *tangawala* (horse carriage driver) because he was whipping the horse so much. She wanted to get off and take a taxi.

Maya was fascinated by places such as the Red Fort, Jama Masjid, the Secretariat, Carol Bagh, India Gate, and Connaught Place. After her stay in Delhi, she went to Agra. When she saw the Taj Mahal, she had mixed feelings. The architects and artists must have been incredibly talented, she thought, but what about the men who brought the marble from the mines of Rajasthan all the way to Agra? Maya thought of slavery, and she also cringed at the polygamy of the Mughal emperor Shah Jahan.

Why did he need so many wives, going even beyond the limit of four wives permitted by Islam? Why did he have so many children from so many wives? Why did he use women as factories to manufacture babies? What happened to his descendants besides Aurangzeb, a religious fanatic and ruthless murderer?

Such questions didn't arise when she visited the famous Har Mandir Sahib gurudwara, also known as the Golden Temple of Amritsar in Punjab. She was amazed to see the long queues of visitors. She was aware that the gurudwaras serve millions of free meals, worldwide and without discrimination. More importantly the gurudwaras served only vegetarian food.

She met two couples who were standing ahead of her in the queue. Amazed by their fair complexion, she introduced herself. She found that they were Brahmins from Kashmir. They called themselves Kashmiri pandits who were forced to leave Kashmir because of intolerant Muslim fanatics.

"There were no Muslim fanatics in Kashmir before India was divided into Pakistan and India. Our parents' Muslim friends used to invite them for meals, and they ate together from the same plate. Kashmiri Brahmins were converted by the Sufis who believed in universal love for humanity." The senior pandit sighed. "After the creation of Pakistan everything changed into hate. So, we are here. My family of ten lives in Allahabad in a two-bedroom flat. We miss our huge house in Srinagar, the capital of Kashmir."

He paused as the other pandit interrupted him. "We are not beggars. We are here to pay our respects to Guru Nanak and the temple. Guru ji was a Hindu like us. He founded Sikhism. One of his missions was to feed poor people without discriminating against them."

"I am aware of the kindness of Guru ji. Kashmir must have many gurudwaras?"

"That is not possible. No one but native Kashmiris can buy property there."

"That's discrimination. I can buy property anywhere in the United States if I have money."

"It's good to hear you speak positively of America. We are aware of the mistreatment of African slaves; but we Brahmins also mistreated our untouchables for thousands of years. You might say we are suffering because of our bad karma. Many untouchables converted to Islam and were happy to make Pakistan their homeland."

These statements from the Kashmiri pandits encouraged Maya to sit with them and eat the hundred percent vegetarian food. The senior pandit explained the principle of *sewa*, a Sikh tradition of service to humanity.

"And service to animals too." Maya was overwhelmed. "Peace be to animals. Peace be to those people who donate enormous amounts of money and food. Peace be to this gurudwara, serving more than eighty thousand meals every day, and on special occasions such as Guru Purnima, Guru Nanak's birthday, over one hundred thousand vegetarian meals!"

"But let me tell you," the senior pandit interjected, "that we pandits of Kashmir are not vegetarians. And we also have some Sikh friends who eat meat—except beef."

"Really?" Maya said in disbelief.

The Kashmiri couples laughed.

CHAPTER SEVEN

MAYA RETURNED TO San Francisco a vegetarian. She told Bijli all about her experience in India. Punjabi vegetarian food was the cuisine she liked the most. "I will miss those delectable Punjabi dishes."

Bijli informed her about a Bay Area restaurant where Punjabi food was served that was run by a Sikh known as Sardar ji, a respectful title (meaning Chief) for any elder male Sikh, such men clearly distinguished by a turban over their uncut hair, unshaven beard, and a metal bangle on the wrist.

Maya visited that restaurant. Maya was convinced this must be a genuine Punjabi restaurant when she heard the devotional song of Guru Nanak that she had heard in Amritsar: "O saint, renounce your mind's ego" (*Sādho man kā mān tyāgo*).

A girl brought a menu to Maya's table. She saw a few vegetarian dishes listed, including some "snacks," spelled *sanaks*. She laughed at the word, which means "whims" in Punjabi and Hindi. She remembered that "school" was pronounced as *sakool* and "spiritual" as *sapritual*!

Most of the dishes served at the restaurant wouldn't be considered spiritual in the sense of gurudwara food, as a bar with an assortment of alcohol was displayed across the dining area.

Maya opened the booklet to find the following:

Beef tikka masala
Beef curry
Karahi beef
Palak beef
Beef samosa
Beef korma
Beef vindaloo
Beef biryani
Egg biryani
Lamb biryani
Palak lamb
Lamb samosa
Lamb tikka masala
Lamb samosas
Lamb saag
Goat Masala
Halal goat meat
Chicken makkhani
Chicken curry
Chicken tikka masala
Chicken saag
Chicken soup
Chicken mushroom
Chicken samosas
Chicken palak
Chicken tandoori
Chicken pakora
Chicken karahi
Qeema naan
Qeema matar

Sheesh kabab
Qeema matar
Palak shrimp
Fish curry
Kashmiri fish
Qeema samosas
Shrimp pakora
Shrimp korma

This list of dishes cannot invoke any spirituality, Maya thought, and she sighed. She couldn't control her anger. She went to Sardar ji, who was sitting at the cash register.

"Sardar ji! I have visited the Har Mandir Sahib. Compared with the vegetarian food of the Golden Temple, your place looks like a slaughterhouse. I became a vegetarian after eating at the gurudwara—"

"We have a whole list of vegetarian dishes. I am happy you visited our holiest temple, but this is a restaurant, not a temple. Our customers love our meat dishes. Have you checked our list of twenty-six vegetarian dishes?"

"I did."

"Which ones would you like to order?"

"Sarson ka saag, makki ki roti, daal makkhani, lassi, and vegetable biryani."

He flagged down a waiter, "Hey, Jagjot! Take this lady's order! The young and beautiful Jagjot came with the menu list in her hand.

"I have already checked the menu." Maya placed her order and Jagjot seated her at a table.

Soon a man served all the dishes Maya had ordered. She found all the dishes excellent. Later, she ordered a *kulfi* ice cream, which was outstanding.

She went to the cash register to pay the bill. "Sardar ji! Your dishes were beyond my expectation. I am sorry, but I was upset because I know a Chinese restaurant here that is completely vegetarian. However,

India, not China, is known as a country of vegetarians. If I had not visited the gurudwara at Amritsar, I would not have been upset."

"I understand," the elderly Sardar ji said affectionately. "My parents were strict vegetarians. After we came here to pursue the American dream, we found that people like our Punjabi cuisine. We hope you come back with your friends!"

"I will. Thanks." Maya got the receipt from Sardar ji and walked toward the door. Jagjot opened the door for her.

"Thanks, Jagjot! I have included your tip in my bill."

"Oh, no! You should have given it to me directly. Dadu never gives us that kind of tip." The word *dādū* means "grandpa" in Punjabi.

"I thought your dadu would share the tip with you!" Maya said when she saw tears in Jagjot's eyes. "Never!"

Maya took three dollars from her pocket and gave it to Jagjot. They hugged each other.

Two years later, Maya and Indira returned to eat at that Punjabi restaurant. It was a Saturday. She did not see Sardar ji or Jagjot anywhere and asked the waiter about them.

The waiter said, "I will tell you their story after you finish your lunch."

Both ordered some new dishes: *Amritsar kulcha*, *raj kachauri*, *chhole*, giant-sized *bhaturas*, etc. After they were done eating, they asked the waiter to pack the leftover food to take home.

Maya and Indira couldn't believe the story the waiter told them then. Sardar ji was in jail. He had beaten Jagjot because he thought she was disrespectful to him.

"Where is Jagjot now?" Maya asked the waiter.

"She never showed up after that incident," replied the waiter.

On their way home, Maya and Indira stopped their car at a railroad crossing where they saw a couple with their four children, three girls and a boy. They became curious because the man looked Indian, his complexion dark brown. The woman was white, and the youngest child, a boy, was in her arms. The man had a small placard in his hand that read in extra-large red letters: Jobless engineer with hungry children.

Indira parked the car at a corner when Maya requested her to give the family their take-home food.

The man thanked the girls and said, "May God bless you!"

"May God bless you, too," Indira said with a smile. "Are you an Indian?"

"Yes," he replied.

"A Hindu?"

"Yes."

"Your white wife is an American?"

"Yes."

"A Christian?"

"Yes, a Catholic."

Maya joked on her way back, "Indira, your Catholic parents have you and your brother only! I don't agree with the family planning minister about his opinion of Indian Catholics. He really met the Pope to get his support, as he joked, 'I am the only heathen who met the Pope for his support for birth control in India.' But the Catholics of India are a minority. It's the majority community that is responsible for the country's population explosion."

"The majority has a tendency to blame the minority for any national failures."

"You are right." Indira nodded in agreement.

"I was in India, and guess what I found. To my surprise, many of the Indian leaders are Hindus, and some of them had over half a dozen children. Among them was a prime minister, and another was a chief minister. They should not have been in power; they should have been in prison."

Indira laughed. "But India's first prime minister, Jawahar Lal Nehru, was a role model. He had only one child, my namesake."

"I got your anachronistic namesake joke, but I agree. Nehru was like a maharaja and could have afforded many children, but he only had the one!"

CHAPTER EIGHT

AT LUNCH WITH Maya and Indira, Bijli picked up Gunanand's memoir about Ismat.

Gunanand revealed he had met Ismat in a Bay Area's Mexican restaurant. At first, he thought she was a Mexican American. Indians look like Mexicans because of the common complexion. In fact, often Mexicans try to talk to Indians in Spanish, mistaking them for fellow Mexicans before realizing they are talking to Indians.

Ismat was from India and called herself a Hindu in front of the restaurant's Spanish-speaking customers. She was actually an Indian Muslim from Moradabad, a town in western Uttar Pradesh.

When she saw Gunanand sitting alone at a table, she stopped cleaning the dining area and set the mop aside. She had no difficulty in recognizing that Gunanand was an Indian, just like her.

"Bhai Sahab, Salam!" She greeted him in Urdu.

"Namaste, Bahin!" Gunanand greeted her with folded hands.

Gunanand was surprised to see such a good-looking and polished Indian mopping the floor. "If you don't mind, I would like to talk to you after I am done eating," Gunanand told her.

When they spoke after his meal, Gunanand was overwhelmed by her story. Ismat was raising a daughter, Rihana, and a son, Jafar.

When her engineer husband, Farooq, was laid off, he decided to go back to India and resettle in his hometown because he had a job offer there. But Ismat refused to return to Moradabad. She said she had several reasons for her refusal and offered up two.

First, she didn't want to face her mother-in-law who disliked her because her parents hadn't given them enough dowry. Ismat was not educated beyond Middle School, and her mother-in-law forced her to wear burqa against her will. None of her married classmates who were Hindus and Christians covered their heads. Worse, Farooq sided with his mother.

The other reason was the future of her two children. She wanted them to stay in the US. and realize the American dream like many other Indians in the Bay Area.

One day, her husband called her from Moradabad. He was accompanied on the phone by a Mullah. She recognized the old Mullah. He shocked her when he said, "Farooq wants to give you *talaq*."

Farooq uttered three times, "Ismat, my wife, I give you *talaq*."

Ismat retaliated quickly every time he enunciated those words by saying, "I too give Farooq *talaq*."

She felt humiliated. "Mullah Sahab, I am not garbage to be thrown out like this. I hope to God that someday India will abolish this shameful humiliation of women and disregard your authority." She hung up.

She found out that the reason for *talaq,* or divorce. was Farooq's plan to marry another woman from his community in Moradabad.

After the divorce, Ismat was forced to leave the Bay Area Indian restaurant where she was a cleaning lady because the manager tried to assault her sexually.

Thus she went to work in the Mexican restaurant, where everyone treated her with respect and paid her extra money to support her two children.

Gunanand was moved when he met her children, who addressed

him as "Uncle." He would meet them occasionally and take them out to watch games like basketball, football, and baseball.

One day Farooq paid a surprise visit to Ismat because he said he wanted to see the children. She snubbed him, and so did the children. So he stayed with an old friend, a classmate from India.

One evening, he threatened her when he found out that Gunanand was very friendly with the children. Ismat informed Gunanand, who understood the man's objection. A parent's meeting with his children must be welcomed, he thought.

Despite Ismat's resentment, Farooq was determined to remain in touch with his children. He knew that the best time to meet them was when they were out with Gunanand.

Such an opportunity arose when Gunanand took the children to a baseball game at Jafar's junior high school. Rihana was twelve years old then and Jafar was fourteen. Gunanand had bought baseball bats and caps for both the kids.

After the game, when Farooq tried to meet his children, they hit him with their bats.

"You trashed my mother in three shitty sentences!" Jafar shouted. "You didn't come for our birthdays. You didn't bring any gifts. Our friends celebrate Christmas and receive gifts. Rihana and I were not so lucky to celebrate *Id* with you."

Rihana spat on Farooq's face when she heard the word *Id* (Eid), a Muslim festival of love, during which *sewain*, a milk pudding, is offered to all neighbors without discrimination.

Gunanand stopped them from insulting their father. "These are your children, and they will forever remain your children, no matter how they are behaving now," Gunanand said to Farooq. "I understand you love them. I love them too."

"Thank you, Gunanand Sahab," Farooq said with folded hands, and then he burst into tears. Farooq clearly showed remorse as he covered his eyes with his hands and walked away slowly.

Farooq never met with his children again.

CHAPTER NINE

GUNANAND GOT THE sad news from Tehri that his uncle, Salik Ram, had died. *He deserved heaven*, Gunanand thought, as he was reminded of his name, Salik Ram. The Sanskrit name *Shāligrāma* is popularly pronounced as *Shāli Grām* in Hindi, and so the people of his Himalayan region often misspell Sanskrit names. Hence, *Shāli Grām* became Salik Ram. A person's name rendered as Salik Ram or his own name as Guna Nand were as fake as such names for the gods as Kedarnath and Badrinath, thought Gunanand. He was, however, not sorry to hear of Salik Ram's death, as he died at the ripe-old age of ninety-one.

Gunanand knew that Salik Ram was disgusted with his two sons but happy with his daughter. Salik Ram's first son, Subal, was an astrologer. He boasted of his prediction that he would get married soon, thanks to his father, who had arranged his marriage despite his objection. He also predicted that his younger brother, Prabal, would remain a *brahmachari,* or bachelor. Indeed, Prabal became a member of an Akahara, or sect, located in the holy city of Haridwar on the banks of the holy river Ganga and all members of the Akhara must remain bachelors. Subal knew the Akhara tradition; members of the Akhara are not to be under the influence of *kāma,* lust.

Subal misguided a couple whose toddler son had cancer. They were told by their doctor that there was no cure for their son, and desperate, they decided to seek Subal's advice. He predicted that their son would be free from cancer if they took him to Har ki Pairi, a famous holy bathing spot of the Ganga river at Haridwar, guaranteeing salvation to the bathers, every day for a bath and put an ash dot on his forehead. Millions of people throng to Har ki Pairi to wash off their lifelong sins by taking a few dips in the river. During the Pot Fair (*Kumbh Mela*), over a million people take a dip into the waters of Har ki Pairi.

When the doctor heard of the Har ki Pairi "treatment," he scolded the parents. "The Ganga is not a holy mother but water flowing from the Gangotri Glacier. Nobody would need medicines or hospitals if glacial waters could cure diseases. No god or goddess can treat your son's terminal cancer."

The doctor didn't want to tell the parents that the Ganga has been a preferred river for suicide. Very often people disgusted with their lives drown themselves in this river. The doctor knew how one of his patients drowned herself because her polygamous father forced her to get married to an old man. The father got good bride price from the old man, who later mistreated her because of the bride price he paid. One day she drowned herself in the Ganga.

'Ma Ganga will never have mercy for the suicide committers' the doctor lamented when he heard about her suicide.

He didn't mean to degrade this great river that created an extraordinary fertile land of the world along with its Himalayan tributaries. Countless men and women, towns, businesses, and schools are named after her and the tributaries. Its famous rival tributary is Yamuna, which also starts from the Garhwal Himalayas. The Ganga meets this tributary, with magnanimity, at Allahabad: the famous place of the Pot Fair (the Kumbh Mela) where the highest number of people of the world meet. It's no wonder why poets such as the Nobel laureate Rabindranath Tagore have honored this river, the river that flows from the high Himanchal (Gomukh) to the Bay of Bengal.

Prabal was horrified when he heard from his brother the dreadful prediction of the doctor. “How could doctors insult Ma Ganga? She was brought down by King Bhagirath from Gomukh where Lord Shiva, out of compassion, released her from his head,” he said to his astrologer brother. “Don’t they know the ancestors of the King were freed from all the sins when Ganga’s waters touched them way down in the worst hell?”

Lord Shiva’s ardent followers are known as Naga Sadhus, naked saints. They mimic Lord Shiva, smearing their bodies with ashes and giving up clothes because they symbolize attachment. They carry iron tridents and paint their foreheads with three horizontal lines of ashes (*tripuṇḍa*). Devout men and women bow to them, sometimes with their heads touching the penises of naked saints.

The glacial waters of the Ganges were flowing from the Himalayas to the Bay of Bengal before humans inhabited India. Even today, nobody has seen any evidence of a chariot driven on the on-foot Himalayan trail leading to the Ganges. The myth of King Bhagirath, travelling to the roots of the Ganges, is clearly a geological joke.

The death of the cancer-stricken boy had not dented the beliefs of Prabal and his brother, Subal. Salik Ram knew very well how his sons deceived gullible devotees by giving them false hope. He wished his sons had become engineers like his son-in-law, a civil engineer in the P.W.D (Public Works Department). The P.W. D. was known to be full of bribe-taking employees, from clerks to contractors, but his son-in-law, Medhavi, was not a corrupt civil engineer. One of his colleagues lived in a big posh house (*kothi*) with four sons and two daughters, all studying in Lucknow’s Convent schools, but Medhavi lived in a small bungalow and had two children attending the Kanpur public schools.

Subal had a back-up profession. He acted as a *panda,* a word derived from “pandit” or “pundit.” The pandas are holy guides performing rituals for devotees at holy places. Subal would take rich devotees to the various holy places scattered all over the Garhwal Himalayas, which was known as the *Deva Bhumi*, land of gods.

One day, during the monsoon season, he took a small group of devotees for the *darshan* of Lord Shiva's *linga* (phallus) at the high-altitude temple of Madhyamaheshwar, locally pronounced as *Madmesur.* The group, during their return, halted at Rudra Prayag, a small town named after the confluence of the Alakananda and Mandakini rivers. A member of the group was swept away by the strong currents when he tried to take a dip at the confluence. Subal jumped into the raging waters to save him, but he, too, was swept away.

A man, a member of the group and a relative of the drowned man, cried out, "How is it that Subal could not predict this tragedy? Is it really Rudra's confluence?" Obviously, his reference is to Lord Shiva, the meaning of the name Rudra, the savior of devotees.

But Rudra Prayag literally means Roaring Confluence, which makes sense, given its noisy fall formed by the two rivers.

When Subal's widow, Tripti, heard about his demise, she wailed. She removed her nose ring, the symbol of a married woman because she was now a widow. She had no children. Who would look after her? She panicked so much that she fainted.

CHAPTER TEN

"MEDHAVI WROTE A long letter to Gunanand," Bijli said to Maya and Indira over lunch. "It was not about the death of his father-in-law, Salik Ram, nor about the death of his brother-in-law, Subal."

Medhavi had tried to persuade Prabal to leave the Akhara and get married to his widowed sister-in-law. Marriage of a widow to her brother-in-law has been practiced from the Vedic times, Medhavi thought. At the time of marriage, the bride is made aware of the mantra *Devṛkāmā bhava*, that is, be desirous of your brother-in-law. This strategy was good so that a widow might be cared for, even though it was uncommon in this Himalayan region.

Prabal became furious when Medhavi proposed levirate marriage to him. "You should know that we Akhara members have taken the vow of *brahmacharya*."

"Why?" Medhavi inquired.

"You quoted the Vedic mantra of *Devṛkāmā bhava*. Let me quote another mantra." Prabal quoted part of the mantra *Brahmacaryeṇa tapasā devāḥ* in anger. "Don't you know our mantra?"

"*Mṛtyumupāghnata*," Medhavi completed the mantra, much to

Prabal's surprise. The complete mantra's meaning was "Gods killed death by the heat of celibacy."

Medhavi's name means "intelligent." He thought at least this stupid Akhara saint must know about the myths of gods.

One popular myth is that Vishnu created the universe.

The ancient Puranic story of this myth shows Vishnu dressed in cotton clothes lying on the cosmic Milky Ocean (*Kshīra Sāgara*).

Miraculously, as the myth claims, Lord Brahmā, emerges from Vishnu's naval while the goddess Lakshmi, Vishnu's wife, sitting near her husband's feet. She is dressed in a sari and a blouse watching the emergence of the four heads and four hands of Brahmā, each hand holding a *Veda*, written in a script! And a wife has to sit near her husband's feet!

The Indian calendars are sold in millions every year with such pictures. The artists of these calendars don't give a damn to what Darwin said, to what biologists, historians, and anthropologists teach in Indian colleges. Even some well- educated Hindus still consider Brahma the father of all beings, and politicians exploit the beliefs of Hindu voters with statements such as, "We believe in Vishnu. We believe in his wife Lakshmi."

Another myth describes how Vishnu married Lakshmi. The gods and demons churned the cosmic ocean, and out of the churning emerged the goddess Lakshmi, one of the fourteen jewels.

She was so beautiful that every god and demon wanted to marry her. Lakshmi was smart. She saw Vishnu, busy in a corner and pretending he was not interested in marrying Lakshmi. But Lakshmi was overwhelmed by the extremely handsome Vishnu, and so she snubbed all the gods and demons. She took a garland in her hand and put it around Vishnu, and thus Vishnu and Lakshmi became husband and wife.

Devout Hindus don't care for myriads of contradicting stories of creation, especially written in Sanskrit, the language of the gods. But they would reject the creation myths of other religions, such as the myth of Adam and Eve. To them, God's original language was not Hebrew or Aramaic; it was Sanskrit!

Moreover, Adam had only one wife, Eve. Lord Ganesha had two wives, Riddhi and Siddhi. Brahmā, too, needed a wife. So, he created, out of his head, a woman called Sarasvati. He married her—his own daughter—who became the goddess of speech and learning.

"Males creating their wives out of their bodies is not a unique feature of Hindu mythology. Even Eve was created out of Adam's body," Maya commented.

"Males have such enormous powers!" Bijli said sarcastically as Indira burst into laughter, ejecting half chewed apple pieces from her mouth.

"The overall point is that God, too, needs sex—a lot of sex. Lord Krishna is God, and he had eight wives, officially," Bijli said, again sarcastically. She was aware of her father's three wives and his brother's four wives—the fourth did not even have a proper marriage ceremony.

Indira showered them with some apple pieces again with her laughter.

"So, what happened to the widow of Subal after Prabal rejected the idea of levirate marriage proposed by Medhavi?" Indira asked when she calmed a bit.

"Tripti, as a widow, was willing to marry Prabal. She had given her consent to Medhavi, who, however, failed to persuade Prabal." Bijli exhaled. After a pause, she added, "So, Tripti went to Mathura, the holy city on the banks of Yamuna and Lord Krishna's abode."

Mathura is known to have a society of widows, all of whom are mostly neglected by their relatives. Tripti joined them and felt good in the company of other widows. One of her best friends was a widow who followed Jainism. "This religion does not even believe in Lord Krishna. There is no God in Jainism," Bijli said.

"She needed a support group. Considering her unfortunate circumstances, she made the right decision," Maya commented. "I hope she is happy in Mathura. Levirate remarriage is not liked by many Hindus. I know a Punjabi student here whose parents were forcing levirate marriage upon him. He flatly rejected their proposal. How could he marry his *bhabhi*, his sister-in-law?! He was bewildered. He respected his widowed *bhabhi* like he respected his own elder sister. But the parents kept pestering him, one letter after another, and one day they found out that he had already married his girlfriend, who was white and his classmate at Berkeley."

"Aren't Sarasvati and Lakshmi shown as white goddesses in our calendars!" Bijli laughed.

"Don't forget the black goddess, Kali, just like me!" Maya joked. "I have seen those calendars in Indian shops."

CHAPTER ELEVEN

BIJLI WAS MOVED by her uncle's memoirs about his friend Dr. Achyut Bart, an untouchable from India who became a gynecologist in the US. Before coming to America, he changed his original name twice. He was born in a suburb of Patna, India. His poor parents had moved there from the Garhwal Himalayas. He modified his community name *Achhut* to Achyut, meaning Unfallen, and Bart is from the Sanskrit word *Vrata*, meaning "vow." Unlike the upper castes, his caste people had no last or family names, just professional designations such as lohar (ironsmith), auji (tailor), and koli (oilman). In Hindi, *Achhut* means "untouchable" or "one belonging to the lowest caste," traditionally the *Shudras*.

As a child he had witnessed how the upper caste Hindus treated those of the lower castes. There was a separate well for the untouchables, and his father was once beaten when he accidentally drank water from the well belonging to the upper castes. In his primary school, Achyut sat in the back corner because a Brahmin teacher had scolded him when he sat in the front bench with high caste students.

As soon as Achyut entered college he came under the influence of Dr. B.R. Ambedkar, the chief framer of India's new constitution, which guaranteed equality to all Indians. Achyut became a Buddhist because Dr. Ambedkar converted to Buddhism along with thousands of untouchables, and he adopted a Buddhist name, Sariputra. And finally he became Achyut Bart.

"Interesting! First, he chose a Buddhist name and then opted for Achyut. Why didn't he keep his Buddhist name?" Indira expressed her curiosity.

Bijli responded, "He liked his Buddhist name as he was a great admirer of Dr. Ambedkar, a role model for socially suppressed people. Dr. Ambedkar was a well-educated politician, better educated than Mahatma Gandhi, Prime Minister Nehru, Sardar Patel—you can name any leading politician or professor of his time. Yet he was humiliated by upper caste Hindus even if they were illiterate. His education from American and British universities didn't count because he was a low caste Hindu. He actually hated this word 'Hindu.' But some fanatics used the word 'Hindu' and *Hindutva* synonymously with Hinduism. However, the term didn't help untouchables. Otherwise there was no need for Dr. Ambedkar to create his Neo-Buddhism."

"But you have not told me why he changed his Buddhist name?"

"He finally realized religion is not the solution but divides people further and creates false hope, not to mention hate. He realized that Buddhism is no exception. He thought that Buddhist nirvana and reincarnation were hoax, as there is no medical evidence of nirvana and reincarnation."

Maya interjected, "I met a Neo-Buddhist in India. He believed in these concepts. Interestingly, that Neo-Buddhist ate meat, ate fish! He was aware of the fact that the neighboring country of Tibet was not known as a country of vegetarians. He also knew that other neighboring Buddhist countries—such as Burma, Sri Lanka, and Thailand—have thriving meat markets."

"Maybe he knew that His Holiness the Dalai Lama ate meat when he was in Tibet," Bijli commented, "and the Lama claims his religion is kindness!"

"That is true of some Tibetans I know. I also know a Thai Buddhist temple here where monks serve meat dishes free of cost to the visitors but donations are requested so that they can feed the hungry. Propagators of cruel kindness! There goes the Buddhist *ahiṃsā*," Indira said.

"I, too, met a Neo-Buddhist. I frankly told him that Neo-Buddhism is not the Buddhism Gautama Buddha had in mind. The disciples of the Buddha could have burned the *Vedas*. Indeed, a scholar like Dr. Ambedkar set a sickening example of burning books. Nevertheless, this man tried to impress me. I understood his veiled intention to convert me. I just joked with him, 'I am a black woman from America. Blacks in general believe in Almighty God. He kept them under slavery for such a long time. Very kind of the Almighty!' The Neo-Buddhist agreed with me on this false notion of Almighty God. 'Buddhism has no Almighty God. You should consider Buddhism.' I didn't want to offend him, and so I said, 'Good. But give me some time. I am in no hurry to attain *nirvāṇa*!'"

Then they discussed how Gunanand liked Achyut's creation of his own Three Jewels when he abandoned Buddhism: I will take resort in humanity; I will not take resort in superstitions; I will take resort in science.

Another experience of Dr. Achyut Bart that impressed Gunanand was about a college educated woman patient whose baby girl died within a week after birth. After three healthy daughters, she wanted a boy, otherwise her husband could divorce her. She believed in Rev. William Golmal's message that "Jesus saves."

Dr. Achyut Bart told her, "Religious freaks can give false messages, false hopes. They can't be held accountable. But if a doctor says or makes any decision that does not work out as intended, he can be held accountable. Doctors can't treat a dangerous disease of believers. It's called 'logical regression.' If we all are the Lord God's children, then why does He let millions of his children suffer and die every year and keep Himself alive forever? Very considerate and compassionate, this Lord God the Father! Religious freaks guarantee meeting Him in His heavenly Kingdom, a place astronomers have failed to find. I have no idea of what kind of rocket science religious freaks use."

He paused because Gunanand was laughing. Then he added, "She didn't seem to be impressed when I told her we need more hospitals, not houses of the Lord; we need more science, not superstitions. Science is not proselytization. Science is salvation. Look, I am a physician who is also a living being. If the doctors can't save someone, then nobody can save that person. No dead person can save any live person. I even dropped a bombshell that it was her husband, not she, who was responsible for the sex of the baby. I also added that in India many believe that Lord Rama and Lord Krishna save people, that prayers to them guarantee the birth of a son. The fact is that their prayers can't change the sex of the baby—and can't save a dying baby either. Despite prayers, in fact, India has an extremely high infant mortality rate."

Gunanand was very sympathetic to Dr. Bart's experience as an untouchable. "In India, *Hindutva* harmed untouchables. We don't need Hinduism; we need humanism. Dr. Ambedkar would not have converted to Buddhism if Hinduism had reflected any sense of egalitarianism," said Dr. Bart.

For the sake of egalitarianism, a couple of relatives of Dr. Bart's were converted by the Aryan Society known as Arya Samaj, which believes that people should "purify" other people by making them "Aryans." They have a Vedic slogan, *kṛṇvanto viśvam āryam*, meaning 'Let us make all Aryans.'

"Hitler would not have agreed with the Arya Samaj because he thought only white people were entitled to be called real Aryans. That insane guy was determined to kill all 'fake' Aryans. Millions of defenseless Jews and gypsies were massacred. When the unreal Mr. God failed to protect them, then real Aryans headed by such outstanding generals as Eisenhower and Patten finished the Aryans of Hitler, the Nazis," Dr. Achyut Bart said. "I feel sorry for those German soldiers who were forced to die for Hitler."

As a doctor, Achyut could not accept the underlying belief of the Arya Samaj that some humans were impure and needed *shuddhi,* Sanskrit for "purification." He called the Arya Samaj purification ritual "false detoxification." God *Paramātmā* should not have created impure human beings in the first place! Or He should have stopped them from being impure!

CHAPTER TWELVE

BECAUSE OF PROFESSOR Murray Emeneau, the University of California, Berkeley, attracted many students, including Indians, to study Sanskrit. Professor Emeneau showed the Indo-European roots of Vedic words whereas Sāyaṇa, the famous Indian interpreter of the *Vedas*, failed to do so.

But Indira was more interested in how the Vedic hymns were recited today in India. She was advised to go to India for a summer session. Some American Sanskrit scholars had recorded the Vedic chants in South Indian temples, and she had already toured a couple of South Indian temples. Some of the pandits there had recommended she visit Varanasi, but when she reached Varanasi, she found it very hot and she changed her plans. Instead, she would visit the Badrinath temple in the Garhwal Himalayas where the pandits trained in Varanasi recited selected Vedic mantras.

On her way to Badrinath by bus, she was mesmerized by the natural beauty of the Himalayan mountains, rivers, and forests, but the Badrinath temple was nowhere as enchanting as the South Indian temples she had seen. Nevertheless, inside the temple she saw a panel of pandits seated way up on a plank. Their Vedic recitation was incredible. She was convinced that this must have been a reflection of the ancient convention of saving the *Vedas* orally as there was no writing then.

At the end of the temple ceremony, she met the Raval, or head priest, who was a Nambudiri Brahmin from Kerala, on the southernmost part of India's coast. In contrast, the Vedic chanters were local Garhwal Himalayan Brahmins.

Indira was shocked to know that the Garhwali Brahmins ate meat and sacrificed goats and sheep to please major gods and goddesses. She inquired of a pandit why the head priest, a Namboodiri Brahmin from the extreme south, was a strict vegetarian and why the Brahmins of this extreme north of India are non-vegetarians.

"We Himalayans are Vedic Brahmins. Various types of meat were part of the regular diet of the ancient Vedic Brahmins and Rishis."

"But your faces don't look like Vedic Aryan Brahmins. I notice certain Tibetan features."

"What Tibetan features?" The Himalayan pandit asked.

Indira did not respond at first. She paused, but when she saw in his eyes that the Brahmin was still waiting for her answer, she resumed talking. "I saw the idol of Vishnu in the temple. His face has Aryan features, a white face. Yours is different, and the head priest's is even more different, a South Indian man. . . Let me change the subject. The temple has idols, but the Vedic religion has no idolatry."

"No, actually we have Vedic temples that have statues of gods and goddesses."

"Vedic temples and statues! The ancient Vedic people had no temples, no statues."

"No, you are wrong."

"Then why is the Aryan Society against idolatry?"

"You mean the Arya Samaj?"

"Yes."

"They are ignorant."

"They are ignorant in one sense. They believe that ancient Vedic people were strict vegetarians. The Vedic people were white people, Aryans, like me. Aryans are not known to be vegetarians."

"Nor are we, the Himalayan Brahmins!" The Brahmin laughed.

After her return, Indira told Bijli about her experiences.

"Your Himalayan region is a natural wonder. I recommend that everyone go for the Char Dham tour of the four renowned holy places."

Bijli didn't react to Indira's praise of these four places. Instead, how her father beat her mother flashed before her teary eyes.

"You don't seem happy," Indira said.

Bijli changed the subject. "Did you perform any *puja* there?"

"Yes, the Raval let me hold the statue of Lord Krishna."

"Did he speak to you?'

"You mean the statue?"

"Yes."

"Statues don't speak."

"Maybe someday I will beat them and see if they curse me!"

"No, you wouldn't do that. Do you think you are like some of those insensitive Muslim invaders who destroyed temples and statues?"

"You never know, Indira. I have my reasons," Bijli said as she wiped her tears.

"You are not an iconoclast. You are a Berkeley Bijli. You are Berkeley lightning!"

"A Berkeley radical!"

"Your name means lightning. Lightning never cries. It roars and burns."

"What would you like me to burn?"

"I would like to see you burn poverty. I cried when I saw the extreme poverty of your people. Worshipping statues doesn't destroy poverty. Statues don't talk to anyone, don't hear anyone, can't even defend themselves. I still wonder at the folk belief of the local people that Lord Shiva and Parvati were married in these Himalayas. Apparently, their son, Ganesha, was born there, too. How come they can't remove the poverty of the local people, their own people? On my journey I saw a few men, poorly dressed, selling cucumbers to the thirsty tourists. I wonder how much money those cucumbers bring!"

"A few pennies."

"I forgot to mention that the head of the Badrinath temple read out the love sports of Lord Krishna, called *lilas*, from the *Bhāgavata Purāṇa.*"

"The *dharmādhikārī* is most powerful and cannot be questioned as to why he is glorifying the love *lilas* of Krishna. These stories encouraged many poets to praise Krishna's love scenes. I have a memoir of my uncle I would like to share with you."

CHAPTER THIRTEEN

THAT MEMOIR WAS about Tanmay Rana, who came from Chicago to visit Gunanand. He taught Sanskrit and Hindi literature at the University of Chicago.

In India, Gunanand and Tanmay were classmates up to high school. Tanmay had a teenage daughter. Gunanand was concerned about Bijli being raised in America and thought that Tanmay could give him some advice because he and his wife Anisha were raising a teenager like Bijli.

"Hey Tanmay, don't you think that Bijli and your daughter should *not* be educated in America?" Gunanand asked him.

"Why do you think so?" Tanmay retorted.

"During the hippie revolution in the sixties, I observed that pornography began to gain popularity. India does not have magazines like *Playboy* or *Stag* or pornographic films. Don't you think our girls should be protected from exposure to such vulgarities?" Gunanand asked Tanmay.

"You mean India is a puritanical country?"

"Definitely."

"In Indian tradition you may not find pornographic films or magazines, but there is no dearth of pornographic literature. Actually, in Indian literature there are no borders between pornography and puritanism."

Gunanand looked surprised by this statement. He had no idea that even the so-called devotional literature contained pornography. Tanmay gave him a few examples to convince him.

"The Sanskrit poetry of *Gita-Govinda* by Jaya Deva is lauded in India, but in Western settings it is considered vulgar." Tanmay then quoted the lines of *Gita-Govinda* about young Lord Krishna's foreplay with his *gopi* girlfriends: *Krishna's both beautiful hands move and massage the plump breasts of the cowgirls.*

Then he added a few lines of Vidyapati and Surdas. Vidyapati wrote in the Maithili language and Surdas in the Braj language of North India. Both men thought they were composing devotional songs about Lord Krishna.

"Just observe these lines of Surdas, wherein he is describing a scene of Krishna having sex with his young girlfriend: *The young boy and girl, holding hands, are absorbed in the joy of intercourse,*" Tanmay added.

"My goodness. These are really obscene pieces!" Gunanand reacted by covering his eyes with his hands.

"You may consider them obscene, but saints like Chaitanya of Bengal used to dance while singing the songs of Jaya Deva and Vidyapati, assuming that their poems were devotional."

"No way. These are definitely pornographic pieces," Gunanand reacted to Tanmay's comment. After remaining silently disgusted for a few moments, his hands over his eyes, he commented, "Surdas lacked common sense. If Krishna was God and Surdas was his great devotee, then how come Krishna could not do him a little favor?" he said as he removed his hands and opened his eyes.

"What favor?" Tanmay asked Gunanand.

"Restore his sight and save him from the torment of blindness."

"Religious faith is blindness," Tanmay responded.

CHAPTER FOURTEEN

GUNANAND TOLD TANMAY how one of his American classmates at Berkeley, a white boy named Bill Sutter, had befriended him. He had told Gunanand that his grandfather, Jon Sutter, was a German immigrant and pronounced his own name as Yon Zutter. Bill was interested in the history of the Maharajas. His father was an art collector and had bought a fancy table that supposedly came from the palace of a Maharaja of Rajasthan.

The only Maharajas Gunanand knew well were the Shahs of the Central Himalayas. He had copies of Shiv Prasad Dabral's outstanding history publications in Hindi that featured the local Maharajas.

Gunanand, however, wanted to check with Tanmay what the difference was between Maharaja and Shah. Tanmay, being a Sanskrit teacher, explained that there was no difference.

"Tell your friend Bill that *Mahā-Rājā* is an Indo-European cognate of Mega-Rex, 'big king.' The Persian word *Shah* and the Sanskrit word *Shāsa*, 'the ruler', are cognates, sharing the same root.'"

"You would like to know about one Shah of Tehri in whose court my great-grandfather was an officer. His views were somewhat different from Dabral's regarding the Tehri Shah, namely Sudarshan Shah. This Shah was good in some ways and terrible in other ways. He was a polygamous maharaja. Officially he had two wives, princesses from the neighboring kingdoms."

"Many Maharajas, like the ancient kings, had several wives. Nothing abnormal about your maharaja," Tanmay commented.

Gunanand continued, "But that lecher didn't stop at two wives. He kept several mistresses called *khavās* women. One mistress trusted my great- grandfather. She had told him that she was not lucky like him and my great-grandmother, just one husband and one wife, dedicated to each other. The Shah treated all the concubines as if they were sex-toys and not as partners. Some he liked and some were neglected. Some were jealous of each other. The princesses hated the mistresses. Those two princesses had no son to rule, and so a son of a concubine had to be designated as the next ruler. There wasn't one son but two—Bhavani Singh and Sher Singh—from two different concubines. Both sons did their best to discredit each other's claim to the throne."

"The Shah sounds like his contemporary, the Nawab of Lucknow. The Nawab had many wives and mistresses. He didn't care for the Islamic limit of four women."

"You are right." Gunanand laughed. "Just like the Nawab, our Shah had good taste in art. He wrote poems, knew music and dance, and even encouraged others to participate in arts and scholarship. My great- grandfather thought that the Nawab was better in a way. The Nawab, unlike the Shah, was not a lackey of the British. The Shah had no intention of supporting the 1857 freedom struggle that the British called a mutiny. The Shah must have felt grateful toward the British, who brought the Kumaon-Garhwal Himalayas back to India from the ruthless rule of Nepal."

"Did freedom from Nepal help women and untouchables? Were they given better opportunities?"

"No Maharaja had ever done so much for them. But one of the Shah's women, Queen Khanet ji, got an opportunity. She and her lackeys plundered the treasury and took away all the precious jewels just when Sudarshan Shah breathed his last. The untouchables were forced to work for minimal wages, not enough for bare subsistence. My great- grandfather wanted to help the poor people, but the treasury had vanished. Nevertheless, the higher castes were able to manage their budgets."

Gunanand thought of Dr. Achyut Bart, an untouchable, who was not impressed by the rule of Lord Rama of the Sanskrit *Rāmāyaṇa* epic. Lord Rama didn't consider untouchables equal to higher castes. Had he considered them equal, then India might have developed an egalitarian culture. He left the *Varṇa* system intact.

Achyut was not among those Hindus who lauded the rule of Lord Rama, known as *Rāma Rāja*.

Tanmay understood Dr. Bart's view. "The disenfranchisement of women and untouchables in ancient times is well known. For example, the Sanskrit dramas make it clear that women were not educated enough to speak Sanskrit; and indeed, only a few men of stature, such as the Brahmin priests or saints, spoke Sanskrit. Women and low caste people spoke in vernacular languages called the Prakrit languages."

"Imagine if the mistresses of the Tehri Shah could read and write in English!" Gunanand laughed. "I wonder if they had any knowledge of the ancient scriptures such as the *Vedas*. Some Hindu fanatics think that women in ancient times were equally fluent in Vedic Sanskrit."

"No way. Women were not allowed to even touch those scriptures," Tanmay said emphatically.

"The Shah used to visit the Badrinath temple where the Brahmin priests chanted the Vedic mantras. To his mistresses, those chants meant nothing. The mistresses and the official queens quarreled over choosing an heir. Look at those two sons of the Shah, Sher Singh and Bhawani Singh! The Badrinath Vedic chanting could not stop their rival ranting. The British did."

"Well, even today those chants mean nothing to most temple visitors." Gunanand remembered how his sister was one of the visitors who didn't understand even standard Hindi, let alone the ancient Vedic Sanskrit. Those chants would have done her no good even if she was able to understand them."

CHAPTER FIFTEEN

GUNANAND SHARED A sad news from his village with Dr. Achyut Bart when he came to visit him on a Sunday afternoon. Latu had passed away. His father Sachchi and mother Asis had named him Gambhir, which means a "serious, thoughtful person." Instead of Gambhir, however, everyone called him Latu, which means "demented." His short tongue, not long enough to articulate words properly, just the sounds *ah ah ah,* disabled him. In other words, his uttered words were so garbled that the listeners thought that he was not fully developed mentally. Physically, his growth was stunted.

His sister Pusi, two years younger than him but much taller, had no speech problems, no communication abnormalities. It was ironic that Latu actually understood what others spoke but others didn't understand what he spoke. Every time Latu needed to communicate, he had to use nonverbal signals. Some of his relatives thought that he was probably possessed by a ghost or a god, and so Latu's parents resorted to shamans, who failed to rectify Latu's speech.

As if this physical handicap was not enough, Latu had another social handicap.

He was born in the *auji* caste of untouchables. Due to the rules of caste segregation, the members of this caste lived on the outskirts of Gunanand's village and earned their livelihood by tailoring and drumming for the higher castes. Latu's father, Sachchi, taught Latu how to play the drum, *damau*, a high-pitched timpani-like drum much smaller than the big bass drum, *dhol*, which Sachchi played with him. Latu could do menial jobs, but he couldn't do tailoring, which convinced the villagers that he was not fully developed mentally. Nevertheless, people marveled at his skill playing complex rhythmic patterns on the drum, patterns that varied according to the ceremonial occasion. For example, there are different patterns to celebrate a marriage than the patterns played on a person's first death anniversary.

Gunanand had some sad memories of Latu's beatings. One day he had diarrhea and spoiled his pajamas, and so Sachchi beat him. Pusi intervened when she heard Latu's cries. She took his pajamas off and cleaned him. It was clear that he was overwhelmed by Pusi's understanding of his problem because he began to weep uncontrollably.

On the celebration day of his niece's naming ceremony, Gunanand sat down to eat food with Latu, the drummer. A higher caste Brahmin like Gunanand was not supposed to touch a lower caste *auji* like Latu, and they were not to eat food together. A male relative dragged Gunanand and threw his food down in a heap. Gunanand couldn't tolerate this humiliation, the humiliation of Latu. He was supposed to drop the leaf plate, full of food, over the stretched palms of Latu—only dropping the plate and without touching him. After all, Latu was an untouchable! A Brahmin would become polluted if an untouchable ate with him, and then he would have to face excommunication.

Gunanand was determined to teach the relative a lesson without any violence. He pulled Latu by his hand and took him all the way to the kitchen, where he ate with him. He announced that Latu would play the *damau* after they finished eating.

Latu played his drum, smiling, all day long.

"Mahatma Gandhi and Dr. Ambedkar would have been so proud had they watched this scene," Dr. Bart said in choked words.

"Let me tell you another story about Latu. This was when we boys were playing soccer. During games, there was no caste-based discrimination; untouchable boys partnered with higher caste boys. Latu would watch us with a look of yearning to play. His actions showed that he understood how to play. When given a chance, he was happy to just pick up the ball from the far-off corners and bring it up to the playground and then kick the ball. Some boys laughed at his poor skills," Gunanand said with teary eyes.

"Many people are evil enough to laugh at the disabilities of others. I can see that you are not one of them."

"You are a doctor. You cannot have xenophobia. You have suffered so much from xenophobic Hinduism."

"Then let us go out and eat good food to cherish your friend's memories."

CHAPTER SIXTEEN

AT THE FOOD Fountain restaurant, Dr. Achyut Bart and Gunanand had a pleasant time discussing the elements of their shared culture that bothered them.

"Your sister was a victim of polygamy. She was mistreated not only by her husband but also his two senior wives. Am I correct?"

"That is why I strongly feel that the United Nations must ban polygamy."

"Actually, there are other versions of polygamy, and I doubt that the U.N. can do much about it."

"I am not sure I understand."

Gunanand was amazed by the story of Dr. Bart's colleague, Dr. Thors, an unethical gynecologist. In America, polygamy is illegal; but Dr. Thors escapes the law quite easily because his polygamy is consensual."

"You mean just like in the Muslim community. If the first wife of a Muslim man has no objection, the husband can take a second wife? It's an illogical custom, this consensual polygamy."

"Now let me talk about another consensual polygamy without marriage."

"That sounds impossible, but go ahead with your interesting story!"

"It's possible but not all that interesting. Patients generally trust their doctors. Failure of trust results in malpractice. But malpractice of some doctors is considered a favor by their patients," Dr. Bart said while scratching his head.

"For example?"

"Normally, a male doctor is assisted by a female nurse when he checks his female patients, but Dr. Thors would take his childless patient to a separate room without a nurse and impregnate her by having sex with her. Since Dr. Thors was white, some childless white women gladly accepted his kind offer."

"I don't believe this!"

"His nurse was aware of this practice of her boss, but she didn't want to lose her job and so she kept mum. She herself was a divorced woman with two children in her custody. She told me that Dr. Thors has fathered at least fourteen children to her knowledge."

"Is he married?

"Yes. His wife does not know, as she is busy raising her four children. She is very beautiful and never boasts of her husband's wealth."

"I think you should do a favor to his wife and suggest she divorce him as soon as possible. He should be in jail for adultery."

"Divorce for her would be a heavy financial burden. She cannot raise four children by herself."

"My goodness! That stupid doctor has fathered that many children!"

"He recognizes only four children as his own, though, the children from his wife. The others don't know about their biological father, namely Dr. Thors."

"I wonder if any of his children would shoot him upon finding out about him."

"So far they simply do not know, and Dr. Thors' practice is going very well. There is a rumor he might run for mayor of our city."

"This adulterous man should never be voted for."

"There are all kinds of voters. A good number of voters would knowingly support adulterous politicians to carry them to a position of power. This is the irony of democracy."

"At least democracy allows us to condemn the adulterous behavior of a politician in power. Think of the old times when a leader was openly a polygamous man but people still praised him. Mythology says that Lord Krishna had eight wives, and yet, even today, Indian devotees are constructing one Krishna temple after another. If you oppose these buildings and call Krishna temples houses celebrating polygamy, you will be criticized. However, if you ask them if they would vote for a polygamous or adulterous man to become their prime minister or president, they would think you are crazy."

"We all tend to justify our contradictions. Don't we?"

CHAPTER SEVENTEEN

AMONG GUNANAND'S MEMOIRS Bijli found a piece of Yashi's diary. Yashi was the daughter of Gunanand's *mausi* (mother's sister), and she sent this piece to make Bijli aware of the predicament of an Afghan girl, Meena. Yashi had met Meena in Delhi and they became friends in college, both working toward their master's degree in economics.

Meena's parents had escaped to India with her when she was thirteen years old. Her parents spoke Dari, an Afghan language like Pashto. Dari speakers are the minority. Meena's parents belonged to the Shia Muslim community and felt tremendous pressure from the orthodox Muslims, especially from their Mullah, not to send Meena to high school. According to the male oppressors, girls were meant for household work and should wear a burqa to cover their entire body. Nevertheless, Meena's parents wanted to give their only child the best possible modern secular education.

The closest inexpensive and, more importantly, democratic country was India and India has been open to receiving Afghan people since forever. As soon as Islam replaced Buddhism, the Afghan women began to experience different values. Islam's ardent followers claimed that their religion was a religion of love, but the fact is that, to date, Sunni Muslims and Shia Muslims don't get along with much love for each other. However, for women, the Sunnis and Shias do not have significant differences as far as their education is concerned.

Meena told Yashi how her parents often cried to go back to their homeland amidst the mountains. The closest mountain range to Delhi were the Garhwal Himalayas, and they visited Karnprayag, situated at the bottom of Joshimath, only once. Joshi Math was too high and cold for them.

But Meena wanted to visit Joshimath and beyond, as far as Badrinath, one of the holiest places for Hindus. She persuaded Yashi to accompany her on this Himalayan trip. Yashi had already seen not only Badrinath but even Mana, the last village in India near the border with Tibet. Meena had heard that there were forests of the majestic deodar trees on the way to Badrinath. Yashi joked with her that those deodar pines didn't have the great nuts of Afghan pines. These Afghan nuts, called *chilgoza*, were a favorite in North India.

Yashi agreed to take a trip in May, when their college would be closed for summer vacation. Meena was interested in meeting the local people and understanding their economy. She spoke Hindi-Urdu fluently, in fact better than most Delhi folks.

For example, many Delhites would say *mere ko patā hai*, meaning, "It's known to me." But Meena would always say the standard Hindi-Urdu, *mujhe patā hai.* Meena's parents often visited Lucknow, where a sizable Indian Muslim community was Shia and their girls had no restrictions to education. The people of Lucknow were known for speaking standard Urdu, not to mention for polite manners and etiquette.

It was the last week of May when Meena and Yashi reached Joshimath by bus. Meena was in awe of the gorgeous mountains. After two days of rest at a small hotel, the girls left for Badrinath by bus on the morning of June 1st.

It was almost evening when their bus arrived at Badrinath. The only place they found to stay was a *dharma shala*, a sort of monastery for pilgrims. The next morning, they bathed and then headed toward the temple. There was a huge crowd on the way. When they arrived near the temple, they found it extremely difficult to move ahead because the visitors, mostly pilgrims, had already jampacked the path to the entrance. The temple entrance was open, and everybody seemed to be struggling to go in ahead of everyone else.

Meena was not enthusiastic to join the entrants and stayed at a distance from the entrance in a vacant corner. Yashi encouraged her to enter the temple, however. "You are a strong girl. Come on. Don't be afraid of a little shoving and pushing."

"I am not afraid of shoving and pushing," she whispered. "What if the priests ask me about my identity? What will happen when I say I am from a Muslim family of Afghanistan? I cannot lie. I cannot pretend to be a Hindu."

"Nobody will ask you who you are, but suppose someone did ask your name. Your name is Meena, which they would think is a short form of Meenakshi, the famous Hindu goddess."

"But I never noticed a Hindu goddess picture or icon in shalwar-kurta!"

"Never mind. Look, so many women are dressed in *shalwar-kurta* and so are you. So am I. Many consider *shalwar-kurta* a Panjabi dress even though this dress came to India via Afghanistan, just like the word *Hindu*. Very much like *Kabuli chana*."

Both began to laugh. It was true that even today those Middle Eastern beans known as *Kabuli chana* (chickpeas) are remembered in India as the "beans from Kabul."

"I know that *shalwar-kurta* travelled to India from Afghanistan and that the ancient Indians never called themselves Hindus, just like our early ancestors never called themselves Muslims."

"Do you think the priests inside have all this historical knowledge?"

"That I don't know. But they can see my fair complexion, hazel eyes, and golden hair, all reasons to suspect me."

"And you are much taller than I am. How tall are you?"

"Five feet and seven inches."

"Four inches taller than me. I am tall enough for a dark-brown Himalayan woman. You are a 'gori,' a fair-complexioned woman. In North India a 'gori' bride is preferred as you must have read the matrimonial ads in our newspapers. Not only ads but even the heroines of films are mostly gori. Even Hindi songs like *'chali gori prit milan ko chali.'*"

"What does that mean?"

"The fair girl has gone, gone to meet her lover."

"Why not a black girl?" Meena laughed.

"Don't laugh at this racist bias of North Indians. One of my cousins was darker than me. She felt depressed because of her dark complexion. She even ordered a cream from a Kanpur company. The company claimed that the cream would change her dark skin into white skin."

"Did it change?"

"Not even a white dot!"

Meena couldn't stop laughing. After a short pause she nodded her head, "I don't want to cause any problems here."

"Alright, if you are hesitant, then we will not enter the temple. Don't worry, even the untouchable Hindus have been forbidden. Can you distinguish me from an untouchable girl?" Yashi asked.

"No."

"Now do you hear the chants inside the temple?"

"Yes, I do."

Yashi said loudly, "Note the hypocrisy of the Hindu caste system! Those chanters are Brahmins. An untouchable man, even if he becomes a Vedic scholar, would not be allowed to join those chanters. Are we really equal in the eyes of God? Lord Badrinath is God. His vision called *darshan* grants the worshipper *moksha*."

"What is *moksha*?"

"Moksha is a hoax. It means 'liberation' from rebirth. There is no rebirth anyway. We humans die like animals, *moksha* forever."

They both laughed.

"Some aspire to be with God after death," Meena said.

"But not with the same God. That reminds me of a quarrel between an Arab Muslim and an American Christian University president. The Muslim could not convince the president that Allah and God are one and the same. The president maintained that his God was not the same as Allah. So, two kinds of God. There is no such thing as one size fits all when it comes to the notion of God."

"Monotheism was invented to fit all."

"Let me tell you a real story of false monotheism. Two years ago, I attended a religious conference. The conference chairman, a Ph.D. in Sanskrit literature, boasted that Hindus believe in one God. Then a man stood up and asked him sarcastically, 'Then why do we have such a huge number of gods?' The chairman quoted a Vedic line which says that the wise thinkers call that One Truth by many names. 'It means all those numerous deities are one and the same,' the chairman explained. You know what! The man got up again and said, 'Sir, you are a Ph.D., and so you have elegant explanations. But don't tell average Hindu like my grandmother that the goddess Sarasvati and Nara-Siṃha, the Man-Loin avatar of Vishnu are two different names of one and the same God!' There was a big roar of laughter in the audience. That silenced the chairman. But the man commented further, 'Fanatics massacred others because of the variety of gods and goddesses. Bring two religions into one space and hate is bound to grow there.'"

"True. Hate grows even within a single religion in the same space. As I said, in Lucknow the Sunnis and Shias make fun of each other."

"Compare them with the Ayyer Brahmins and the Iyengar Brahmins in South India. They hate each other. For the Ayyers, Badrinath is Vishnu, who is not God. Their real God is Lord Shiva, who lives in the temple of Kedarnath. But for the Iyengars, Lord Badrinath is Vishnu and the real God. Different enclosures for God, the Omnipresent."

"Like the Sunni mosque and the Shia mosque in Lucknow. Different enclosures for Allah, the Omnipresent."

The girls decided not to enter the temple. Instead, the next morning, they proceeded to the Mana village on foot and reached there in the afternoon.

They stopped at a teashop where a sign proclaimed it the last teashop of India. They enjoyed the tea and the spicy hot *pakoras* while watching the sky-kissing, snow-clad mountains in front of them.

When Meena noticed about half a dozen women passing by the shop carrying loads of fuel woods on their backs, she asked, "Who are these women?"

"They are Tibetan Indians. Very poor people. Lord Badrinath, who resides within a walking distance from here, hasn't helped them. Their ancestors have been here for centuries. They are Hindus by religion, but they are distinguished as the *Bhotia* people. *Bhot* or *Bhotant* is another name for Tibet."

"I am a lucky woman. I came to India all the way from Afghanistan to study. These women should be given an education."

"Some men from their community do get an education. I know two *Bhotia* boys in my high school. Those boys were toppers, so brilliant."

"I wish a great future for their daughters," Meena said with folded hands.

As soon as they came out of the teashop, they saw four women in ochre robes. One woman was helping another young woman, who was limping. Each had a walking stick. Meena became curious. She asked Yashi, "Who are these women?"

"They are called *jogini*, which literally means *yogini*, a female yoga practitioner, but they are actually nuns and collect alms for their monastery. Sometimes arrogant men make fun of them in Garhwali, and some have been raped, even by their fellow monastery monks. The monks appear holy with their ochre robes and colorful forehead marks, some pretend to be holier by smearing their bodies with ashes, but these are not holy men."

"Can we talk to these *jogini* women?"

"Let me try."

Yashi went forward and, with folded hands, greeted them respectfully with the words *Māī jī praṇām*, meaning "(Holy) Mothers (our) special bow (to you)."

"*Āsirbād*," pronounced the senior-most nun. The Sanskrit word *āśīrvāda* for "blessing" was mispronounced, exhibiting her poor knowledge of Sanskrit. It is not uncommon that many monks and nuns, in spite of their ochre robes, mispronounce Sanskrit.

"Where are you coming from?" Yashi inquired.

The senior-most nun replied, "We went up to the Basudhara and bathed in the big falls' current."

After visiting the Badrinath temple, some pilgrims go a couple of miles up on foot from Mana, closer to the Tibet border to take a holy bath in the icy waters of *Vasudhārā* falls, assuming that it washes all their sins away. This fall's water flows down the hill and merges with the Alakananda. Slightly wet clothes on their bodies made it clear that the nuns did bathe, but they were not shivering as it was, fortunately, a sunny day and only slightly breezy, indicating that soon the monsoon rains would hit this region.

"Does she have a problem walking?" Yashi pointed toward the limping woman.

"She is gasping for air. Basudhara was too high for her," the senior nun responded with a sigh.

Yashi understood her problem. The falls is situated at a higher altitude than Badrinath, and no doubt, pilgrims who are not natives of this region suffer from low oxygen levels in their blood.

"You need some pickle. Do you have some with you?" Yashi inquired.

"No."

"Let me take you in the teashop," Yashi invited them, and the women followed her.

Since Meena was curious about these nuns, Yashi requested the waiter bring tea, *pakoras*, pickles, etc. out to a corner.

The nuns seemed very happy with this courtesy. The senior nun kept looking intermittently at Meena. Yashi thought she might agree to give an interview to Meena.

"My friend Meenakshi is interested to know about your lifestyle."

Meena pressed her lips to stop herself from smiling as she heard the name Meenakshi.

The senior nun looked at the other nuns with a smile. They all smiled, indicating their agreement. Being *joginis*, they were expected not to lie, and the revelations from their interview shocked Meena.

One woman became *jogini* because her husband used to beat her often, sometimes with a piece of firewood. Another woman was raped by a man, and afterward her in-laws and her husband turned her out, assuming that it was her fault. The senior-most nun had no children and was a widow. She took refuge in the Srinagar monastery. The woman who had problems because of lack of oxygen became a *jogini* because she was born under a constellation of stars (*namli*) that made her marriage chances virtually nil.

After the tea party was over, the senior nun got up and said, "Thank you for your kindness. Now we have to leave to attend the evening *arti* of Lord Badrinath."

Meena and Yashi bid them farewell. Surprisingly, the limping nun was not limping anymore.

Meena and Yashi took out some money from their handbags and called the waiter who served snacks.

The waiter looked stunned. "May I ask you what your business is?" he asked while folding his hands as if he was going to cry, obviously overwhelmed by the generous tip.

"We are college students," Yashi replied. "What is your name?"

"He smiled. "They call me Badru. My full name is Badri Dutt."

"That means gift from Lord Badrinath. Right?" Yashi asked.

"Not right when someone becomes mad at me and calls me a 'gift from Bandri,' or a 'gift from a female monkey.' If my mother were a monkey, she could have made some noises. If there Badrinath Bhagwan was really sitting in that temple, someone must have heard him speaking but nobody has recorded a word from his dumb statue. If he had any power, then I would not be a waiter. Instead of cleaning the dirty floor here, I could have gone to college like you."

Two men at a table beside them overheard him and started laughing.

After leaving the teashop, Meena didn't look happy. She remained nearly catatonic for a while. Yashi broke her silence. "Meena, why are you so quiet and look so sad?"

"I feel sorry for that waiter. But he is lucky he is here where he at least has the freedom to say there is no God, no Badrinath, no Bhagwan, out loud. If a Badruddin had said that openly in Afghanistan, he would be in deep trouble."

"Our economics professor says that openly. He says that human activity is driven by economic needs. Even religious faith is motivated by money. He is right. The temple priest down there doing *arti* needs money. Those who are chanting *arti* need money."

"I hope Lord Badrinath's fiery *arti* burns the bad kismet of those women."

"I feel sorry for that limping girl, that *namli*. Badrinath is Lord Krishna, who married repeatedly. He could have given her at least one chance to marry. I wonder what kind of god she is worshipping! Badrinath has no power over anybody's destiny. Badrinath is not *Vishal* or 'Big.' Lord Badrinath can't even remove the poverty of the people of the little Mana village within walking distance of his temple. Dumb devotees can't see this little area around Badrinath mired in all kinds of miseries. Instead of that temple, a college could have helped that waiter," Yashi commented.

Meena nodded and said, "At least that waiter is not a beggar. Far back in Afghanistan's history, when Buddhism arrived, people became familiar with Buddhist nuns and monks. The monks were known as *bhikkhu* and the nuns were known as *bhikkhuni*—"

"I know those Pali words derived from the Sanskrit *bhikshu* and *bhikshuni*, literally meaning 'beggars,'' Yashi commented.

"I understand this lifestyle must have become attractive for lonely women and removed the chances of homelessness; being a nun offered not fake *nirvana* or *moksha* but real social, economic, and emotional support."

"I agree. We have no record of those nuns who might have encountered the same circumstances as these *joginis* did. The dead Buddha has no power over their destiny. But at least Gautama, the Buddha, did exist—unlike Lord Badrinath."

"I have been told that the Buddha accepted untouchables in his Order. Anybody like the Buddha?"

"Yes. An example is Swami Dayanand who founded his own Vedic organization. called the Arya Samaj. The swami treated the untouchables like the Buddha did in his Order. I tell you an Arya Samaj story from the town of Pauri, where an Arya Samaj Brahmin of Garhwal began to eat regularly with the local untouchables. One day some upper-class Hindu boys of Pauri threw stones at him. 'I am trying to remove the shameful sin of segregation of thousands of years' he yelled at them loudly. They yelled back at him with obscenities. He also retaliated with foul words of Garhwali and Hindi. Their opposition, however, could not prove as a deterrent. He continued his reform without any rituals, such as purification mantras. I think he was influenced by Mahatma Gandhi. The Mahatma used to treat untouchables with equality and without idolatry. The whole world knows the Mahatma as a reformer, but not this little Garhwali Brahmin. We don't know how many little reformers have been ignored in history." Then she revealed, "Meena, my parents were caste-segregationists. They hated the Arya Samaj, because it opposed idolatry. From the point of view of the Arya Samaj, idolatry is non-Vedic. The Badrinath and Kedarnath temples promote idolatry."

"Muslims in North India call the idolators But-parast."

"Which means the 'Buddha-followers' in Farsi. Isn't that

interesting that the statues of the Buddha have big international market?"

"But nothing like the greatest rock statue of Afghanistan!" Meena stared at the sky raising her hands straight up. "Visitors from all over the world come to see that Rock Buddha!"

"Someday, I would like to see that wonder of Afghanistan with my own eyes, Meena."

"We will go together." Meena said with teary eyes.

CHAPTER EIGHTEEN

THE NEXT SATURDAY, Gunanand invited Dr. Achyut Bart for lunch near his home in a Bay Area restaurant.

Both ordered vegetarian dishes. Achyut joked, "We are eating vegetarian dishes. I have met some hardcore fans of Vedic rishis in Bay Area. They don't take me seriously when I tell them that Vedic rishis ate beef."

"My professor friend from the University of Chicago, who teaches the Vedas, can give them a list of meats the Vedic rishis used to eat. The Vedic rishis didn't have a real sense of the sanctity of life. They didn't have the social ideals of educating the Shudras and women. So he called them 'racist' and 'misogynist' saints. Just for a moment, imagine if Bijli was born during Vedic times and there was a Berkeley type gurukul, a guru's school. Bijli would have had no chance to be a student of that school." He quoted an ancient Sanskrit prayer that the teacher and the student used to say together, *Saha nau bhunaktu*.

"I have heard it being recited when Dr. Ambedkar was fighting for the education of the lower castes. Also, I had challenged a *Hindutva* fanatic once about the prayer, 'Let us eat together.' Prove that the guru and the student were two women or two Shudras when praying. Or prove that the teacher was a Brahmin man and the student was a Shudra boy studying the Vedas together. Hindu fanatics cite a couple of names of learned Vedic women and then generalize saying that most Vedic women were learned."

"Dr. Ambedkar's movement convinced me that we don't need Hinduism. We need *humanity* instead. Religion divides; humanity unites. Religion accounts only for its followers, whereas humanity accounts for everyone. Based on this illogical discrimination, the rishis divided India. 'The dumb rishis were not true educators,' says my educator friend. 'A true educator would give equal chance to anyone interested in education. Race, religion, caste, gender, country do not matter to a true educator.'"

"How many Shudra boys like me must have cried as they watched the upper-class boys studying under the guidance of Vedic rishis. How many parents of the Shudras must have felt gut-wrenching pain and humiliation that their children would never have the same opportunities as the Brahmins, Kshatriyas, and Vaishyas! Those racist rishis were xenophobic, as they defied the natural way of reproduction. They would not allow a Shudra man to marry a higher *varṇa* girl or the other way around. Otherwise, they believed, an inferior race would be the undesirable outcome. Why the hell do we call these stupid rishis seers? Fanatics see the elegant words of the rishis, not their discriminatory actions. I am appalled when the fans of the Vedic culture fail to mention the social injustice and pain inflicted by the Vedic racist rishis upon those who were labeled as Shudras by no fault of theirs. Where are the Vedic mantras that record the pain of the Shudras?"

"I agree. '*No Shudra child deserves education* was the ideal of the ancient rishis. It was a cultural degeneration that hurt the progress of knowledge. The rishis made a fool of their phony *Vedānta* philosophy that all is *Brahman*. If all are your own selves, then you should have educated your other selves, the Shudras, too,' says my educator friend."

"Thanks to the modern educational system established by the

British, we untouchables can seek higher education. And now I can record my pain and humiliation."

"If the Vedic rishis were fair minded, then today India would not have to face the question of 'affirmative action'. Hindu fanatics don't realize what the hell the caste system based on the *varṇa* system caused to India."

"The priests fool the public even today. They perpetuate the caste system as part of the *Sanātana Dharma*, the senior religion. Segregation forever. India was divided by the creators and supporters of the caste system. It's a shameful partition of humanity."

"I have to tell you the experience of my mother's sister. In her village they had a priest with a big family, seven children. Mausi told me how those children would play with children of other castes of her village. They did not follow the caste barriers. One Sunday afternoon, the older boys of her village were having fun playing soccer. Accidentally, a boy, who was the goal-keeper, bumped his head against the goal post made of hard raw oak. His head started bleeding. The eldest son of the priest tried to stop his bleeding using his handkerchief. He wrapped it around his head to stop the bleeding while uttering the Vedic *mahāmṛtuñjaya mantra*. The repetition, called *japa,* of this prayer mantra supposedly overcomes *mṛtyu* 'mortality.' In the evening, when the priest heard that his son had uttered the holy Vedic mantra in the presence of an untouchable, he became so furious that he began to slap him. His wife tried to stop him, but he started slapping her, too. My *Mausi* heard her screams and ran to stop the priest."

"That priest should have realized that, if religious witchcraft can treat wounds, then we would not be needing medicines and medical professionals."

"The priest believed that mishaps in a person's life are the result of bad positioning of the nine planets in one's horoscope, and so the priest used to recommend a remedy, worship of the planets, known as *graha pūjā*. Apparently, each planet needs proper food items to be pleased. For example, the sun is pleased with the offering of a big packet of white rice, as the Lord Sun's color is white. Lord Saturn is black in color and so he needs a big packet of black beans. The priest collects these items offered by the troubled person and enjoys them later in his kitchen!"

"I know. Thank goodness that, for the untouchables, the planets and their worship are too far!" They both laughed.

CHAPTER NINETEEN

AT A LUNCH meeting, Bijli discussed with Indira and Maya the bitter dispute at the United Nations between India and Pakistan over Kashmir. Both countries claimed all of Kashmir, which was divided between Pakistan and India. Pakistan's contention was that Kashmir's majority population was Muslim, and so it must belong to Pakistan.

"Uncle Gunanand, when he was a student at Berkeley, participated in a small meeting about this dispute. If you are interested to hear a different perspective regarding this dispute, then I have a memoir of my uncle. This is about a meeting sponsored by the South Asia Program chaired by Professor Gumperz."

Upon hearing the name of the professor, both took an immediate interest in the topic.

Mr. Jay Shukla was a young faculty member in the Sociology Department at IIT Lucknow. Berkeley invited him to be a speaker at the Forum of South Asia Program. Ironically, he was a staunch Brahmin raised in a family that followed the line of the political party known as Jana Sangh. Later, the Bhartiya Janata Party emerged as an avatar of Jana Sangh and was run by anti-Muslim Hindus.

The attendees at this meeting counted not more than a dozen, mostly Indian Hindu students and one Muslim from Allahabad. This Muslim student, Jawed Rahman, was a history student at Berkeley. Since the group was small, each student got up and introduced himself by his name.

Unfortunately, Jay Shukla ended the meeting on a bitter note by talking about India's problems after the creation of Pakistan in 1947. There was no Pakistani student at the meeting. Nevertheless, he offended Jawed in his speech, emphasizing that Pakistan was created for Indian Muslims but most of the Muslims chose to stay, illegally, in India.

During the question and answer period, Mr. Shukla and Jawed engaged in a heated debate.

"Mr. Shukla, do you think I am staying in India illegally? I was born in India like you; I am very much an Indian like you!"

"Mr. Jinnah founded Pakistan for Indian Muslims. So, yes, if you consider his partitioning principle, then no Muslim should be given Indian citizenship."

"Sir, this is the standard principle followed by all civilized countries: a native is automatically a citizen of his or her birth country. You are denying me my birthright."

"Muslim cultural values are different. They are not Indian. Pakistan's official language is Urdu. Indian Muslims have sympathy for Pakistan because of similar values."

"I am a history student. Urdu is the same language as Hindi. The Hindi language that you and I speak was standardized by Indian Muslims, not by Hindus. Any professional linguist will tell you that the use of two different scripts does not make a language two different languages. You and I speak the same language, and I can use both the scripts. I am sure your father must have used both the scripts, since your birthplace is Aligarh. Am I right?"

"Yes, not only my father but even I use both scripts—Devanagari as well as Arabic."

"Let me add," Jawed said, "that you and I enjoy the same music, eat the same kind of food, play the same games, watch the same movies, and so on. How are my cultural values different from yours?"

"Muslims believe in polygamy. A Muslim man is allowed to have four wives. Harem is not an Indian value," Mr. Shukla said.

"Harem was not started by Muslims. Any historian will tell you that harem was allowed by religions much older than Islam. Among those religions is Hinduism, which is the oldest. Even some ancient Hindu rishis, not to mention Hindu kings, had multiple wives. As for me, my father had only one wife, my mother. My grandfather, too, had only one wife, my grandmother," Jawed said with a victorious smile that made the audience laugh.

Gunanand interrupted. "My father, too, had one wife and my grandfather had one wife. But unfortunately, my sister was married to a man who already had two wives living under one roof."

The audience laughed.

"It certainly sounds like a laughing matter, but it was not so for my sister. I don't want to discuss her married life here, but I do want to tell the audience that Jawed is right. Islam did not start polygamy. I also agree with Jawed that any person born in India has the right of Indian citizenship—"

Another Indian student interrupted Gunanand. "I beg to differ with Jawed, as well as with the distinguished speaker. To be an Indian, you don't have to speak the same language, eat the same food, play the same games, and watch the same movies. Look at our faces. Such a small gathering. Yet, do we look similar from any angle? And don't forget Jim Corbett, a white Indian, who hunted man-eating tigers of Garhwal and Kumaon hills."

The audience applauded. One student shouted "Yes, we all are together and equal partners."

Another student, unusually tall and burly, got up and said, "The speaker should realize that India is not a monolithic country. Its diversity is well known. Jawed is a representative of that diversity. The Parsis, the Jews, the Tibetan Dalai Lama and his followers who were persecuted in their own lands—all found a safe haven in India. The speaker is misrepresenting India. He better shut his mouth—"

Professor Gumperz intervened. "It's alright to express our opinions freely. After all, India and the U.S. are democracies, not dictatorial countries."

His statement seemed to be directed toward Pakistan, which was run by military dictators, a situation the founder of Pakistan would never have recognized.

After the meeting was over, all of the Hindu students surrounded Jawed to thank him for his statements. Gunanand, too, complimented his statement on Hindu polygamy.

"Jawed, you might have heard about Sudarshan Shah, the Maharaja of Tehri. He had two queens and many mistresses. After his death, the chosen heir was the son of a mistress. The Shah had another son from another mistress, and the two bastard sons of this Shah struggled to be recognized by the British as the new maharaja. Unlike the last Mughal heir, Bahadur Shah, their father, Sudarshan Shah, didn't want to join the 1857 Indian Mutiny to free India from the British Raj. I doubt Sudarshan Shah considered himself an Indian."

"I know that, unlike the Maharaja of Kashmir, the last Maharaja of Tehri was forced by his subjects to join the Indian Union. Many Maharajas sought British protection, as if they had bought their kingdoms from the British," Jawed said.

The tall burly student patted Jawed on his back with a smile. "Jawed, you should have asked the speaker, 'Has your daddy bought India from the British?'"

CHAPTER TWENTY

ONE OF GUNANAND'S entries in his memoir was quite sad and an eye-opener in Bijli's opinion. The memoir contained a letter from Chaiti, the same woman who had written to Gunanand to help Bijli escape her father's clutches. During the next lunch meeting with Indira and Maya, this letter became the topic of discussion.

Gunanand had an aunt, his father's sister, named Harshi who had two daughters. Harshi had raised them by herself because her husband died of heart attack just after the birth of the younger daughter. The elder daughter, Sandhya, was much older than the younger daughter, Bhavani. Harshi lived in her husband's village, which was situated at the foot of a hill. The village was tiny. The families of her husband's cousins and their children lived in the same village. All the families owned substantial land, including many terrace fields. However, they had to bring potable water from a creek about a half a mile from the village. It was the women's duty to bring water from the creek. Bhavani started carrying water when she was ten years old.

One early morning when it was still dark, Bhavani left for the creek to fetch water. While coming back with the big water container on her head, she slipped and fell over a thorny bush. A thorn pricked her eye and blinded her. Since then, her second name became Kani, which means "blind," and was used when someone wanted to reprimand her or merely taunt her.

"That's awful!" Indira exclaimed.

"It's cruel," Maya hissed.

"However, she was functional, as her other eye was fine," Bijli said.

"You mean, even after the incident she was sent to bring water from that creek?" Maya asked.

"That wasn't a burden for her. The real plight began after Sandhya got married. Traditionally, the married girl lives in her husband's house. This was not the case for Sandhya. There is another tradition which allows the married girl to continue living in her paternal home. However, her husband, too, lives with her and owns her 'house' and considers her property his own. Such a husband, therefore, is called *ghar jamain*, which literally means 'in-house son-in-law.'"

Maya and Indira could not control their laughter upon hearing Bijli's translation of *ghar jamain*.

But Bijli didn't laugh. "This tradition turned out to be unfortunate for Bhavani when Sandhya gave birth to a son. Bhavani's chores increased with his birth, so much so that one day she ran away and became a *jogini*. You remember what a *jogini* is?"

"Like the ones Meena and Yashi met?" Maya asked.

"Exactly," Bijli responded. "Upon their return from Badrinath to Srinagar, those girls spotted Bhavani at a temple festival. This festival is quite funny. The head monk of the temple called *mahant* is smeared with ghee. The devotees lift him on their shoulders and dance. This ritual is known as the 'play' of the head monk. The devotees feel blessed when they touch the ghee-soaked *mahant*. The *joginis* can also touch him for his blessings."

Maya and Indira laughed again.

"Bhavani, too, tried to touch his eyes, hoping that her blind eye would regain sight. One man slapped her and shoved her out of his way. That's when Meena and Yashi spotted her. They persuaded her to return to her village. She did return, and Sandhya was very happy to see her back because she needed help raising her son, Pravin. When Pravin was five years old, his tonsure ceremony exacerbated Bhavani's misery. The priest who performed the ceremony was also an astrologer, and he predicted that Bhavani would regain sight in her blind eye if she went to the nearby Chandrabadni temple and offered the blood of a sacrificial animal, preferably a goat. Sandhya arranged for the sacrifice despite Bhavani's objections. She ignored her objections and brought a goat one day."

"No kidding!" Indira exclaimed.

"The following night, when everybody was asleep, Bhavani ran away from the house carrying the goat. It was pitch dark. She tripped over a rock on her way to the mountain temple and fell in a ravine where she died. The goat ran away. Her goal was to pray to Goddess Chandrabadni not to accept that defenseless goat's life."

"You mean a goddess seeks the sacrifice of innocent beings?" Indira asked.

"Priests are clever. All they have to do is utter a mantra and pour water in the ears of the animal. If the animal shakes its head, then the priest announces that the deity has accepted the sacrifice. The man standing beside the priest with a big dagger in his hand chops off the head of the animal immediately. The devotees shout, 'Victory to Mother Chandrabadni.' Then an *arti* plate full of lighted ghee-soaked wicks is circulated. Some devotees put coins on the plate. Some simply bow with folded hands." She paused and then continued, "The priests here are ignorant. They don't see any contradiction when they peddle the fiction that these hills are the land of gods. India's ancient word for non-killing is *ahimsa*. But *ahimsa* has no value in this land of gods!"

"Who is this Mother Chandrabadni?" Indira interrupted as she shook her head.

"Her Sanskrit name is *Chandravadinī*, which means Moon-Faced Goddess. She is Lord Shiva's wife, the same as Parvati, the

Mountain Goddess. Recently, I heard the news that they have now banned such a sacrifice, but too late for my uncle's dead cousin." Bijli sighed.

After a grim pause, Indira questioned the usefulness of soaking the head monk in ghee: "Ghee, or clarified butter, is a healthy food. What a waste of food!"

"The letter contains the same question posed by Yashi, a student of economics. Her professor was disgusted with religion. He considered religion a sickness that exacerbated national poverty. Millions of tons of ghee is wasted in *arti* and *havan*. Millions of tons of ghee is used to cremate dead bodies in the open. Live bodies inhale the smoke inadvertently, not realizing that any smoke is a pollutant and a health hazard. In a poor country like India, this concept of burning ghee must become the burning topic of discussion."

"Wastage of edible food is a crime, and this crime must be stopped," Maya suggested.

"Instead of stopping it, devotees build more and more temples where ghee is used in every *arti* and every *havan*. The craze of temple building is a waste of national resources in Uncle Gunanand's opinion," Bijli said.

"Why didn't he raise his voice against temple building?" Indira asked.

"He would have been eaten alive by religious fanatics," Bijli responded.

"That can be called spiritual cannibalism," Maya commented in a light-hearted manner.

CHAPTER TWENTY-ONE

ANOTHER SAD ENTRY in Gunanand's memoir was an unexpected letter from Ruchira after a hiatus of many years.

"Dear Gunanand ji! My name is Ruchira. If you remember, we were together at Berkeley. You, Preet, and his wife Naina sang a song at our party one evening, and after the police officer came, we had to stop the noisy *bhangra* dance! I will write more if I hear from you. I live in New Delhi now, not Rampur."

Gunanand immediately remembered her delicious *kari*, which everybody had enjoyed except Liz. He also remembered Bhanu, who had been planning to marry Liz despite having a wife and a child. That had bothered him, and so he made an anonymous call to Liz telling her that Bhanu was committing bigamy and the wedding never took place. Gunanand also remembered how he had joined Preet and his wife in their song. He hadn't liked Preet's behavior, as he had glared at his wife when she forgot a couple of lines from the song.

The flood of memories prompted Gunanand to acknowledge Ruchira's letter immediately, inquiring about her husband, Ram Jas.

Ruchira was delighted by his immediate response, and she wrote back to him:

"I am delighted to hear from you, Gunanand Bhai. You inquired about my husband. He battled cancer for a long time, and by God's grace, he passed away peacefully. After his death, I moved to Mumbai with my elder daughter. By God's grace, her husband is an I.A.S. Deputy Commissioner. The other son-in-law, by God's grace, is a lawyer in Lucknow. I will write again soon. God bless you. Your old bhabhi, Ruchira."

Gunanand was disturbed after reading her letter. He wanted to write back, expressing his anger over the premature death her God had blessed her husband with. But he thought it inappropriate, and so he wrote a short condolence letter instead.

Bijli mentioned this letter to Maya and Indira. They, too, seemed to share Gunanand's annoyance.

"How does she know that God did this and that?" Indira wondered.

"Hindus have many gods. Maybe one god did 'this' and another did 'that,'" Maya commented. "I thought that Ruchira, being a woman, would have believed in Goddess or *Devi*, not in God or *Bhagwan*. When I was in India, I visited a Durga temple where some of the worshippers thanked Durga, the Mother Goddess, for the favors bestowed upon them. A woman swore that *Bhagwati Durga* blessed her in her dream."

"My guess is that, because Ruchira lived in the U.S. for quite some time, where 'May God bless you' is a common expression, she must have picked up the habit. And now that she was living in India, she couldn't let go of the habit."

"Regardless, Uncle Gunanand didn't like her thanking any god she meant," Bijli reacted. "She could have written, 'I am sorry to inform you that my husband passed away long back. However, you would be happy to know that my son-in-law is an I.A.S.' Why give credit to deities!"

Bijli tilted her head back and looked at the white ceiling. She wondered if she should tell Maya and Indira what favor the Shaivite

God, Kedarnath, and the Vaishnavite God, Badrinath, did for her mother.

Indira and Maya looked puzzled when they saw tears in Bijli's eyes.

"What's the problem Bijli?" Maya asked.

She lowered her eyes and said, "Nothing."

"No, no, you have to tell us why you are sad," Indira insisted.

"My late mother might have thanked God if my father had died before her. That old man is still alive."

She wiped her tears.

CHAPTER TWENTY-TWO

BIJLI HAD NO desire to see her father, but she changed her mind when she received a letter from Chaiti. Apparently, her father was suffering from arthritis and he very much wanted to meet his daughter.

Two months after receiving the letter, Bijli flew to India. It was dark when she arrived in her village. Quietly, she entered the room of her father.

"Papa, I am Bijli. I am here to see you. How are you doing?"

"Oh, my darling! Welcome home! You have grown up, my beautiful daughter."

Bijli didn't greet him in the traditional way, that is, by touching the feet of elders. The father and daughter continued talking in Garhwali.

"My mother was beautiful, too. And she died. She was much younger than you, and you are responsible for her early death."

"Let us not talk about sad things. I want to live to see your marriage. I want to see you being carried away in a beautiful *doli*; it may add more years to my life."

Bijli got annoyed by the word *doli*, the palanquin used to carry the bride to the home of the bridegroom after the wedding ceremony.

"I don't want your dream of watching me in a *doli* to come true. I want my independence, not *doli*. A bride is not a give-away object to be carried away in a place unknown to her. My mother was sent away in a *doli* only to be beaten like a cow by a bully husband."

She picked up the bamboo cane lying beside her father's bed. "This is my whip now!" She flashed the cane and hit him several times.

He cried out in pain.

"All polygamous men deserve to be beaten," she said in response to his screams.

When she stopped hitting him, she saw two pictures hanging on the wall. One was of a spring night when Lord Krishna danced with young girls, the cowherd *gopis*, along with Radha, who was presumably present without the knowledge of her husband. The other picture was of a festival in which men rode elephants followed by barefooted beautiful maids carrying baskets of flowers. Apparently, the artists never thought of these colorful pictures as representative of male superiority. Bijli began to hit those pictures furiously.

"Dear Bijli, please don't hit Lord Krishna's picture. I beg you to stop your absurd lashes."

"I am going to destroy your polygamous role model."

She hit and hit and hit until the picture fell to the floor and broke.

"There goes your Hari's harem! Down with polygamy! Down with the slavery of women. Down with the Almighty Avatar and His myths created by men! I wish my mother were alive to watch me. Her return from pilgrimage was blessed by your beating. You believed Tulsidas, a racist and misogynist poet who justified beating women and Shudras like drums. A woman is not a drum. A Dalit is not a drum. Now it's my turn to treat you like a drum. I have returned from my American pilgrimage to bless you."

"Hindus will curse you. Stop your absurd attacks!"

"I am not afraid of their curses. They won't feel my mother's pain. They didn't come to save her, a defenseless devout Hindu woman. Not a single Hindu god, not a single Hindu goddess came to save her." She hit him again.

"You know why?" She hit him again. "Because those deities never existed. Ma came back from her pilgrimage. She was late by two days because of the landslide. Badrinath and Kedarnath can't stop recurring landslides and deaths of pilgrims. Now try praying to those non-existent deities!" She hit him again.

Bijli unleashed her wrath, inflicting more pain upon her father with a few more lashes.

"Remember, you have already given me away by beating me."

Then she left the room. As planned, she went straight to Chaiti's home and knocked the front door.

"Who is it?"

"Aunty, I am Bijli, daughter of Shyamal contractor!"

Chaiti opened the door. "My God, I could not have recognized you."

Bijli touched the feet of Chaiti.

"May Almighty God give you long life."

"Aunty, thanks for your blessings, although I destroyed the Almighty just before coming here. But I need your blessings. I am hungry," said Bijli, panting heavily.

They went to the kitchen where Bijli drank a glass of water. Then they quickly fixed a dish—*basmati biriyani* mixed with a couple of vegetables. Chaiti served it with *chutney.*

After they finished eating, Chaiti said to Bijli, "Tell me about your experience in America."

I will tell you tomorrow. Can I sleep here tonight?"

"It's your home, my dear Bijli *beti.* Let us sleep now. I am alone here. Tomorrow morning, the young girls of our village will come to drop flowers. You know tomorrow is the last day of the spring festival."

Bijli nodded. She had deliberately planned her visit to coincide with the end of the festival.

CHAPTER TWENTY-THREE

SHE WOKE UP the next morning when a batch of little girls arrived at the door, all with baskets of multicolored wild Himalayan flowers. One by one, every girl dropped some flowers on the doorstep of Chaiti's house.

Bijli opened the door when she heard the knocks. She dropped an American penny in each girl's basket. "This is American penny, girls!" she said with a smile. "A shiny copper penny brings good luck to the receiver."

The girls were overjoyed. Their boisterous utterances woke Chaiti. She partly overheard Bijli's conversation with the girls. As soon as she came out of her room, she announced, "Do you girls know who this kind woman is?"

The girls had no idea that this woman had avenged her mother last night. They shook their heads and said in a chorus, "No."

"She is Bijli, the lightning of our village, born and raised here; but now she lives in America."

The girls looked at Bijli in awe but left as soon as they saw another batch of flower girls approaching the house.

After lunch, Bijli took a small gold statue out of her handbag and handed it to Chaiti.

"This is my gift for you. I have not enough words to thank you for saving my life."

Chaiti burst into tears. Bijli wiped her tears.

"Tell me about this statue."

Bijli told her about the revolutionary American woman who started the fight for women's suffrage. "Her name is Susan B. Anthony."

"I have heard about her, but I don't deserve this expensive gift. It is made of gold, after all."

"Actually, it didn't cost me a penny. I have several American classmates who contributed to the purchase. Two of them have Indian names. One is called Indira. As you must have guessed . . ."

"After Indira Gandhi," Chaiti quickly responded.

"The other is Maya. Both are aware of Indira Gandhi's hero Lincoln, the great U.S. president, because he fought against the slavery of black people. Lincoln did not wait for the help of the non-existent Almighty. Maya believes in Lincoln but not in the Almighty. She told me that, if the Almighty existed, he would have stopped slavery right in the beginning. Black people go to churches but don't ask where the coward Almighty was hiding when defenseless Dr. Martin Luther King was being beaten, when his defenseless follower John Lewis was being beaten. Nelson Mandela is not known as a great follower of the Almighty. Why should he be? For letting him rot in jail for twenty-seven years?"

She paused and then added, "As a couple of ancient Sanskrit sayings go, *Only by hard work things are accomplished. Only powerless people worship God.* Mahatma Gandhi must have known these sayings. When defenseless Gandhi was being beaten while working in South Africa, where did his fair Almighty God Rama disappear then? Come on Mahatma! Be a rationalist! It's your effort, your hard work that freed India without the tools of terrorists, without bombs and bullets."

"You are right," Chaiti said. "The Almighty loved segregation for thousands of years, loved the suppression of powerless people. Only by human efforts is segregation coming to end. There was never a single flower girl from our neighboring untouchable community. Rama or Krishna didn't treat them as equals. My Brahmin father told me that Almighty God Krishna claimed in the *Bhagavad Gita* to be the creator of the caste system."

"Many idiots believe that we all are God's children, and so all equal. But not those untouchable girls," Bijli added. "God must be an idiot to have idiot children like Hitler. Like father like son."

She paused again and then continued. "The claim of the *Bhagavad Gita* is false. The Indo-Aryans, long before the *Bhagavad Gita*, had already established this discriminatory division of humanity as stated in the world's first scripture, the *Rigveda*."

(The "Hymn of Man" or *Puruṣa Sūkta* of the *Rigveda* is a well-known reference used to justify the slave status of the Shudras.)

This was a revelation to Chaiti, who wasn't fluent in Sanskrit. She was impressed by Bijli's knowledge, but at the same time she was shocked to know that Bijli became an apostate after going to America. If Bijli had not gone to Berkeley her story would have been different.

"How do you know so much?" Chaiti asked Bijli with awe.

"My late Uncle Gunanand taught me. His Sanskrit professor friend at the University of Chicago helped Uncle understand the ancient cultural matters of India."

"Your late uncle? You mean Gunanand is dead? That's very sad news."

"Don't feel sad. He will live through his memoirs. One day I am going to publish them in their entirety."

In the evening Bijli and Chaiti took two big pots of *basmati biriyani* and went to the village of the untouchable tailors (auji), who traditionally earn a living sewing clothes and playing the *dhol-damau* drums. Lately, many young untouchables had abandoned these traditional professions as India adopted the policy of 'reservation' (affirmative action) to educate them.

"Let us sit down and eat. We have brought leaf plates." Chaiti opened the pack of plates made of big flat leaves of giant *malu* creepers.

Initially, the untouchables hesitated to eat with Bijli and Chaiti. "You are our guests," Bijli said with folded hands. Then she served them the *basmati biriyani* and *chutney*.

They ate together, praising the delectable dish. They savored the rice preparation with hot and sour *chutney*. After dinner, they decided to assemble in the small soccer field for the young untouchable boys. Four untouchable men brought out their drums, the *dhol* and the *damau*.

They started with the famous Garhwali song created and composed by Keshab Anuragi, who had an M.A. in Hindi, wrote his songs in Hindi, and become famous across the country. Not many knew that he was an accomplished player of *dhol-damau* as well. He was usually seen in pants and shirts, sometimes wearing a necktie, too!

These illiterate drummers, who were dressed in Indian pajamas and Western shirts, were totally at ease with Anuragi's Garhwali song.

Hey dīdī hey bhulī hey bwārī
Haryū haryū ghās hwe ge palī raulī.

"Hey elder sisters, hey younger sisters, hey sisters-in-law!
Green grass has spread across the banks of the other rivulet."

This was a song to welcome the spring. Green grass was needed to feed the cattle. The women would get more milk if they fed the cows with lots of green grass.

All the drummers joined the lead *dhol* singer. After finishing the song, they engaged in a friendly drumming competition; the drummers smiled as they looked at each other. Two young tailors joined the drummers with their bagpipes, which the people in this region had inherited from the Scottish army employed by the British in these Himalayan hills.

Suddenly, one *dhol* player lifted Bijli up on his shoulders and started playing his drum louder. He was followed by his fellow musicians and they danced in a circle. Bijli threw flying kisses and slapped her thighs, and the audience laughed at Bijli's movements, which they had never seen before.

Everybody kept dancing until late into the night, and then they left for their homes.

Before going to sleep, Chaiti inquired, "Bijli, I noticed that, while you were throwing kisses, you were slapping your thighs and murmuring something. What did you mean?"

"I enjoyed the drummers beating their drums, just like I enjoyed beating my father last night. I was not murmuring. I was screaming at the top of my voice: *Women! Wake up! Don't believe any polygamist lecher religious leader! He used women for his lust under the garb of that garbage called religion. Beat the damn polygamist, dumb dumb dumb.*"

CHAPTER TWENTY-FOUR

BIJLI STAYED WITH Chaiti for a week. They shared many stories, and Chaiti slowly, but coherently, began to reconstruct her memories. Memories of Bijli's polygamous ancestry, the untouchable cook's experiences, Rangini's visit and her experiences, and many other big and small events in Bijli's village. The experience was revelatory for Bijli.

"I know about your Kandyal male ancestors who had three to four wives in their harem," Chaiti said with a smile.

"Harem! That's the enslavement of women. It's so outrageous, so infuriating! How long has the Garhwal Himalayas had this shameful tradition?" Bijli inquired as she spread her eyes wide with disgust.

"There is actually no such tradition. Your male ancestors were among the few to practice it," Chaiti said. "The great grandfather of your father was the first."

Then Chaiti began to narrate a sort of *Genesis*. "The first known male ancestor of Bijli was Ram Bhakt, which means Rama's devotee. Ironically Ayodhya's King Rama had only one wife, Princess Sita. Ram Bhakt's fourth 'wife' was not really married to him. He just brought her home with the agreement of her parents. The agreement involved bride price and her poor parents needed the cash. In other words, Ram Bhakt bought his fourth wife Prema with no Hindu marriage ceremony. Everybody in the village thought that she was a maid. Within a year she bore Ram Bhakt's son, named Damodar. Ram Bhakt had one daughter from his first wife, and Prema was younger than that daughter. Ram Bhakt already had two sons, one from the first and another from the second wife. Because the senior wife considered Prema and Damodar 'illegitimate,' they were forced to live in a nearby village where Ram Bhakt owned some land.

"When he was a man, Damodar became a police officer. He arrested two innocent Nepalese farmhands in Garhwal who had gone back to Nepal to visit their families without informing their Garhwali employer. Damodar remembered recent history, when the Nepalese Hindu Gorkha army massacred the people of Garhwal and Kumaon hills. They abducted many men and women and took them to Nepal. The people of the region of Garhwal and Kumaon were very grateful to the British who brought their region back into India.

"One night the two farmhand Nepalese somehow managed to free themselves from the small prison of the small Garhwal town of Pauri, where the British maintained a sort of headquarters. Instead of fleeing they went to the house of that police officer, Damodar, and murdered him in his sleep. Then they fled.

"The rest of the property of Ram Bhakt was divided among the two senior sons. One of the sons died. He had no children, and so his property was owned by his other senior sibling, Murli Mohan, who also had four wives. Why not! The Hindu Avatar Murli Mohan had several wives and girlfriends.

"Bijli's grandfather was Murli Mohan's son, Parvati Bhakt. Murli Mohan claimed that Parvati blessed him in his dream with a son, and Parvati Bhakt literally believed his moron father's claim. So, he would participate in any worship or ceremonies dedicated to Parvati.

"Parvati is Lord Shiva's wife from the Garhwal hills, and hence she is called the Mountain Goddess. But Indian devotees call her the World's Mother (Jagat's *Jananī*). Some people visit these hills to see her.

"However, none of them has claimed yet to see her living here or in any other part of the world! Parvati Bhakt had various beautiful human pictures and statues of this goddess in his house. It didn't bother him that those pictures were the creations of human artists and full of all sorts of folk myths.

"He never understood why in many popular pictures and icons Parvati is Gauri, a white woman with an Aryan face. Why do most Tibetan-looking Brahmins of these Himalayas relate their ancestry to the Vedic sages, who were pure Aryans? It didn't occur to him that, if Parvati was a Himalayan woman, then like typical Himalayan women she also should have some Tibetan or Chinese features.

"He was awed by her outstanding body covered by clothes and ornaments, including a costly golden crown, a shiny nose ring, two shiny big earrings, a half-sleeve blouse, and a thin colorful sari as she stood barefooted in the cold Himalayan mountains. For him she was *Shaila Sutā*, Mountain's Daughter, an extremely cold father's child and so cold didn't make her uncomfortable.

"Like many devotees, he never questioned her birth from a mountain! If she was Mountain's Daughter then her children must be mountains, not humans. Instead, she became the mother of humans and not of other creatures! He could have taken her as a 'woman born in the mountains.' Or, like men and women born and raised in the Himalayan mountains, she also eats meats. If so, then animals must be sacrificed in her Himalayan temples and their meat must be served as her blessings. He liked his priest's rationalization: 'The sacrificial animal is very fortunate to be served as her meal. There is good karma for such animals, and good karma for the attending devotees who get to eat free meat!'

"Priests would never tell devotees that statues or icons of all deities observe everlasting fasting and silence, never move by devotion of any kind, that they are in fact unable to recognize who the hell the devotees or priests are.

"Before breakfast Parvati Bhakt would offer the goddess a prayer with a *jap*, holy repetition, of her one thousand names,

Sahasra-Nāma, such as *Devī*, *Bhagavatī*, *Hemamālinī*, *Hemavatī*, *Karuṇā-mayī* or the 'Kindness-covered' etc. Sometimes, if in a hurry, he would silently pronounce her 108 important names using a rosary in his hand. He would offer such a silent prayer during the sacrificial ceremony while the priest was conducting the sacrificial prayer loudly.

"Every year Parvati Bhakt would be a participant in *athwar*, the cruelest animal sacrifice. This sacrifice has been credited to her name *Mahishasuramardini* "Buffalo-Demon Beater." He firmly believed her ancient myth: she killed a human-eating, awful-looking demon named Mahisha or Buffalo.

"So, in the annual ritual of *athwar,* this Buffalo-Demon Beater goddess finds that demon again. A male buffalo is designated that demon. The ceremony starts in a temple, not with any dance but with ear-piercing mantras, bells, and conchs. Anybody is allowed to enter the temple except the untouchable castes, even though the temple was built by the untouchable people who live in segregated houses or separate villages. Their villages are called *dumana* or *domana,* colony of the *doms.* The word *dom* for the untouchable is *doma* from which the word Roma for Gypsies is derived. The Sanskrit word for *doma* untouchables is *Shudra*. That the *Jagat Jananī* World's Mother treats her children unequally is beyond the understanding of the upper-class Hindus. There are also no women allowed inside the temple on this occasion, and of course women on their period are not allowed to enter the temple on all occasions. The drummers of the *dhol* and *damau* are untouchables of the *auji* caste. They beat the drums in front of the temple entrance.

"Anyway, the mantras induce a trance in some devotees, who shout '*hoot hoot*' to draw the attention of other attendees or to show off their superior devotion. Some of these goddess-possessed persons don't even understand Sanskrit, the sacred language of the mantras. But the priest knows that the standard ancient scripture *Manusmṛti* 'The Laws of Manu' forbids killing animals for eating their flesh. If a person, for example, kills a goat then that goat will kill that person in its later incarnation. The *Manusmṛiti* concept of such a karmic role reversal of predator and prey continues life after life because a person eats the meat of different animals on different occasions. Obviously, Manu, the presumed author of *Manusmṛti*, didn't have the advantage of modern biological knowledge. The karmic law, 'all have to pay for their sins,' is considered a pillar of Hinduism. But Manu ignored the commonsense advice given by an Indian atheist hundreds of years before him that there was no rebirth possible after the body is reduced to ashes. But regardless, the participants in this ceremony, like Parvati Bhakt and the priest, don't care about karmic law. They are not afraid of the death that the sacrificed animal will inflict upon them in its next incarnations.

"The last part of the ceremony includes *arti*, which consists of lit ghee-soaked wicks on a metal plate. The ghee, clarified butter, could be from cow milk or buffalo milk. While the *arti* plate is moved around the statue of the goddess, the devotees sing the praise of the goddess. The priest places a red mark on the forehead of every attendee, which symbolizes the blessing of the deity. That mark is also offered to the drummers outside. The drummers consider the mark an honor and feel blessed.

"Ironically, the designated buffalo, eating grass outside in the temple yard, apparently not apprehensive of the imminent danger, looks relaxed and undisturbed by the deafening sacred noise inside the temple. He doesn't understand that the noise of the conchs is meant to invite fun-loving people of the adjacent villages.

"But soon the buffalo is forced to run, as if he is afraid of the invisible goddess. Devotees run after that beast while beating him with swords. He bleeds, writhing in excruciating pain until he dies. His big horns provide no defense against his human predators. His dead body does not go to waste because the low caste untouchables like the buffalo beef.

"Of course, Parvati Bhakt knew that buffalos are vegetarians, not cannibalistic demons, and don't kill humans or any other animals.

Actually, down in the Gangetic plains, their necks are tied to a yoke and they are goaded with a whip to pull a plow.

"Why does the goddess kill such helpful docile animals? Why doesn't she kill very dangerous animals such as tigers, cobras, bears, cheetahs, etc.? The concept of *Ahiṃsā*, non-killing, was obviously not part of Parvati Bhakt's philosophy.

"And his linguistic information was also very limited. Why is this goddess's name not found in other languages such as Hausa, Hebrew, Hittite, Hottentot, Hopi, and etc.? Aren't these languages of *Jagat* (the world)? Why is this mother of the universe not mentioned in other world religions such as Judaism, Christianity, and Islam that forbid the worship of statues?

"Parvati Bhakt has watched her dances, including the Indian classical Bharatanatyam, a dance style common, but far from Parvati's Himalayan home, in the far southern states of India. The intricate movements of the Bharatanatyam dance for Parvati on the icy floors of the Himalayas would obviously be very risky—chances of slipping! Nobody has claimed yet to have seen her dancing anywhere in the Himalayan terrain.

"In the northern states this dance is accompanied by the tabla drums and harmonium, which are not used in the authentic Bharatanatyam. The tabla drums were invented by a Muslim musician of Delhi. And the harmonium is a French invention. The instrument has bellows like an accordion and keys and reeds like an organ. In short, this kind of dance and music didn't originate in the Himalayas.

"Once Parvati Bhakt became mad at a visiting anthropologist who dared to debunk such ahistorical or mythical traditions that Parvati Bhakt, like other dumb devotees, took for real. The anthropologist understood that those devotees wouldn't give a damn about geology, biology, and astronomy. He was not an anthropologist who believed in cultural relativism, but he knew if anthropologists criticized such cruel traditions, they might not get the cooperation of their native informants!

"Nevertheless, later that anthropologist talked to the Badrinath's temple priest, a Nambudiri vegetarian Brahmin from the far southern coastal state of Kerala. This priest remained silent, afraid of the local meat-eating Brahmins who believed that their ancient Vedic Brahmin ancestors had approved animal sacrifice and enjoyed that animal's meat called *kravi*. The anthropologist failed to convince the Nambudiri priest that the Badrinath temple was not a Vedic temple, that in fact there were no temples in Vedic times, just special sacrificial *Vedikā* altars.

"He, however, was happy when the priest took him aside and whispered, because he was afraid of the local meat-eating hill Brahmins, that he didn't approve of animal sacrifice, that a law to ban animal sacrifice was needed, and not just in these hills but everywhere. He quoted a mantra from the *Yajurveda* that says: 'See all the beings with friendly eyes.'"

Then Chaiti told of the exchange between the two: The anthropologist said, "I have some questions for you, sir!"

"Let me ask my local assistant pandit if he would like to take care of your questions," replied the Nambudiri priest. "He is a local Brahmin who comes here to recite the Vedic mantras." He got up and talked to the assistant pandit.

The pandit did agree to talk to the anthropologist. They went out in the backyard and sat down on the knee-high wall of the yard.

"Pandit ji, my American name is too difficult to pronounce. Just call me with my adopted Indian name, Kedar. Kedar ji. I thank you very much. May I know your real name, Pandit ji?"

"My local family name was different. My father changed it to Sharma. Most Pahari Brahmins have Sharma as their horoscopic name. You can call me Sharma."

"All right, Sharma ji. The Nambudiri Brahmins are South Indians. I was in Mysore where I met a non-Brahmin man of my age. He was very friendly and told me a joke. You may not like it."

"What was the joke?"

"My friend took me around that beautiful South Indian city,

a very clean city. On the way he told me this joke. Suppose if you see a cobra and a Brahmin together in a place. Whom should you kill first? The answer is clear. First the Brahmin." He paused momentarily and then asked, "What do you think of this joke?"

"It's a racist joke."

"My friend told me that less than ten percent of the population in the South are Brahmins. But they dominate, and discriminate against, the majority, the non-Brahmins. You are right. It's a racist joke. Brahmins would not marry a non-Brahmin as if the two are of different races."

"The same is true here in our hills. We Brahmins do not marry a non-Brahmin. Brahmins marrying Brahmins made all hill Brahmins relatives."

"Now I would like to change the topic. Let me ask you a funny question. Would you allow the untouchables to enter a temple?"

"No," Sharma ji responded with a nod.

"Who makes the temple?"

"The untouchables."

"Can they touch the icon of the goddess sitting in the inner sanctum of the temple?"

"No. The icon is consecrated with a life-establishment ceremony."

"What is this ceremony?"

"It is an elaborate ceremony that makes the icon to have *prāṇa*. That's breath."

"Did any doctor check to see if that icon was breathing?"

"We never check with any doctor. It's just our Hindu tradition. All our new temples anywhere have to have this 'life-establishment' ceremony called *prāṇa-pratiṣṭhā*."

"Is a woman priest allowed to perform this ceremony?"

"In our hills priests are male."

"Why not female priests? Don't mothers keep us alive right from the beginning, right in their wombs?"

"Women go through menstrual cycles, which makes them impure for the job of temple priest."

"Pandit ji, if there were no menstrual cycles, human life would not be possible."

"I understand your point. Women are allowed to do other kinds of worship, but not the Vedic ones. The life-establishment ceremony is strictly Vedic. And in our hills, we adhere to the Vedic tradition. You must have heard the Vedic recitation at the Badrinath temple. The reciters are all male Brahmins."

"But the Vedic Aryans were not idolators."

"That I don't believe."

"Sharma ji, I assure you that no doctor, Indian or non-Indian, would consider any idol a living being, with a ceremony or without a ceremony. And no doctor would consider any woman impure."

"Do you have any other questions?" Sharma looked somewhat uncomfortable and impatient.

"Yes. Do you use cow urine during that ceremony?" The anthropologist had noticed Sharma's impatience, which he ignored.

"Yes, in our hills *gomūtra* or cow urine is a common item in our *pūjā*. That is, in our worship fresh cow urine, not any other animal's urine, is considered sacred. The cow is like a mother because she gives us her milk."

"How about a she-buffalo? I know that she-buffalo milk and its ghee are as popular as cow milk and cow ghee. And Mahatma Gandhi used to drink goat's milk. He treated his goat like a mother."

Sharma couldn't stop from smiling. That made the anthropologist somewhat relaxed. So, he dared to ask the pandit, "Sharma ji, do you drink the ceremonial cow urine?"

"Yes. It helps to remove impurities."

"Did any doctor tell you this is so?"

"No."

"Can any untouchable bring fresh cow urine for the ceremony?"

"No. We don't allow that. The untouchables are not offered the sacred drink anyway."

"By the way, did you ever have a headache?"

"Yes."

"Did you check with a doctor?"

"Yes. He gave me aspirin. It worked."

"Aspirin is a Western medicine, not Indian. It doesn't discriminate against anyone, Indian or non-Indian. But the cow urine discriminates. It is not good for the impurities of an untouchable, and not good for a white American like me either. I don't understand such a discrimination. Why?" the anthropologist asked with a blink coupled with a smile.

The pandit stopped talking and walked away.

Chaiti revealed how the pandit turned out to be her relative. He told her about his encounter with the anthropologist. He also told her that his boss, the Nambudiri priest (Raval), didn't approve of animal sacrifice and hunting animals for food or game. Chaiti felt emboldened. She began to encourage her fellow villagers to become vegetarian like her and protect the wildlife of the Himalayas. Some of her devout relatives criticized her with counter examples. King Rama of Ayodhya didn't hesitate to engage in hunting, called *mṛgaya* in Sanskrit, they told her. King Dushyanta, the father of King Bharata, after whom India is called Bharat, came to Garhwal for hunting. Chaiti rebutted these references by saying that Kaṇva, a vegetarian sage, objected to Dushyanta's killing the deer of his hermitage.

Bijli encouraged Chaiti, "Just ignore your critics. You have the right to free speech. You have the right to debunk religion. Otherwise, no reforms are possible if we don't protest. Tell them to send their girls to school. Teaching girls how to pray is not going to improve their future. Reading, writing, and science would."

"I agree with you. Daughters are considered 'liabilities' and boys 'God's blessings.' I have heard stories of parents who kill their baby girls. In the womb or outside the womb, it's murder."

"A caveat. A warning. For girls. Seek freedom from veils. Open your eyes and mouths freely. Raise your voice and shout like hell. Feticide is crime, a crime against humanity."

CHAPTER TWENTY-FIVE

CHAITI CONTINUED THE *Genesis* of Bijli's ancestry:

Bijli's grandfather had four wives in his harem. The first wife died with a miscarriage. Then he added three women to his harem. The second wife, an exceptionally pretty woman, gave birth to four sons and two daughters. A male (*bhūt*) and a female (*aheṛī*) ghost bothered her whenever she was with her husband. They would be knocked to the floor by the ghosts. Some of her relatives asked her what the ghosts looked like. 'Their feet are turned backward, and they always wear white clothes to match their white faces. They are quiet. Nobody would hear them. They can walk in the air.' Many others claim to have seen such ghosts, and the neighbors enjoyed her ghostly experiences.

The local folklore gives many reasons for being a ghost after death, but the most touted reason is that those humans become ghosts who are not given proper funeral rites. A murdered person would become ghost and then haunt not only the murderer but his whole family. One remedy to get rid of them is to invite a shaman into the home of the haunted person. The shaman's sacred language is not Sanskrit, the language of the gods. He shouts in a mixture of Hindi and Garhwali at the haunted person while playing a drum, threatening to touch the body of the haunted person with a scorpion plant twig (*kanḍaḷi*), which causes blisters that produce excruciating pain. The haunted person cries, but the shaman assures the audience that it is the ghost crying.

Another popular remedy is to read *Hanumān Chālīsā*, a booklet consisting of forty couplets by the famous poet Tulsidas, who claims that no ghosts would come close when one utters the name of Hanuman, the famous monkey who helped King Rama, the hero of the *Rāmāyaṇa* epic. Like Rama, Hanuman spoke Sanskrit. Many so-called Brahmins can't read and write Sanskrit. They better do better than Hanuman, the most revered monkey! How Hanuman, a speaker of ancient Sanskrit, can understand the modern hybrid Avadhi language of *Hanumān Chālīsā* is also a miracle. King Rama died thousands of years ago, but not his servant Hanuman, That's also a miracle. Hanuman is seen once in a while by fortunate devotees, but only in India and Lanka. Why Lanka, the beautiful island country near the Indian southern coast? Because that's where Sita, the wife of Rama, was imprisoned in a beautiful garden by Lanka's demon king Rāvaṇa.

Demons, too, spoke Sanskrit. They tortured Sita because she was not willing to marry Rāvaṇa. Like Rama's father Dasharatha, this demon king believed in polygamy. Ironically, none of the four sons of King Dasharatha followed the disastrous tradition of polygamy. With the help of Hanuman, Lord Rama was able to locate Sita and eventually killed the demon king and his demon army and Rama regained Sita safely. Then he and Sita flew back to their capital city of Ayodhya in a plane owned by Rāvaṇa.

Hanuman has no family of his own because he remained a bachelor. Those who try to insult this monkey god can face him and his monkey party. The monkeys may bite those who insult Hanuman but not eat their flesh because monkeys are strict vegetarians. Otherwise, Hanuman is known for his humility. He never boasted that he helped Rama. He always remained a very selfless servant of Lord Rama. Untouchable shamans don't worship this monkey god, nor do the strict followers of the Vedic religion. Like King Rama, Hanuman is not a Vedic god. Nevertheless, there are Hanuman temples everywhere, not only in these hills but in other parts of India as well. But the devotees of Garhwal believe that Hanuman has special connection with the Garhwal Himalayas, although this is not mentioned in the *Rāmāyaṇa*. They firmly believe that Hanuman came here for special life-saving herbs. Indeed, Himalayan herbs have always been in demand for Ayurvedic medicines.

Those herbs were needed to save the life of Rama's brother, Lakshmana, who was critically wounded by Meghanāda, a son of Rāvaṇa. Who prescribed those herbs? It was not a shaman but a Brahmin doctor of Rāvaṇa. After all, doctors observe no borders; every patient is treated without discrimination. This great ideal is put forward in the third largest epic of the world, the *Rāmāyaṇa*. Hanuman flew all the way to Garhwal from Lanka and then flew back to Lanka across the sea, and within a day, to save the life of Lakshmana.

Thus, a rich folklore evolved, with which Chaiti was familiar. Hanuman's statues, icons, and pictures are usually painted in red, like the red faces of rhesus monkeys. The *Rāmāyaṇa* story says that monkeys built a bridge between India and Lanka.

Chaiti's father told her that to date no civil engineer has been able to build such a marvelous sea bridge! Devotees literally believe the *Rāmāyaṇa* as a history book, not as a story book. So, Hanuman is a god, a very good god. There is evidence. No animal sacrifice is allowed in any Hanuman temple, just like in the temples of King Rama, who hunted deer, though. Some of Rama's devotees don't support the use of venison and deerskin. The worship of Hanuman can be performed anywhere in any language—no temples necessary. On the other hand, a shaman may ask to sacrifice a cock or goat or sheep to please the haunting ghost. The shaman gets the biggest portion of the sacrificed animal. No ghosts or any gods or goddesses have been observed eating the sacrificed animals! The Hanuman folklore is not a shaman's choice. There is no mention in the *Rāmāyaṇa* story that Hanuman fought any ghosts or Hanuman ate any animal meat!

Chaiti continued.

Bijli's father, Shyamal, was the fourth son. The first son, Devi Prasad, was a forest contractor. The second son, Chandra Dhar, was a court officer clerk called Munsif. The third son, Ramapati, joined the Indian British Army.

Chandra Dhar and Ramapati had their own checkered pasts. Chandra Dhar's first wife had a son, Shuk Deva. Shuk Dev lost his mother when he was two years old. The following year, Chandra Dhar got married to a second wife who gave birth to a son. When Shuk Dev was thirteen years old he ran away because his stepmother had been mistreating him. Shuk Dev was never found. Chandra Dhar married a third wife who had two daughters and he treated them as servants, like farmhands.

Ramapati went to fight in Germany. He was very proud of his military adventures and used to tell his friends about them. One is very graphic. Two young German soldiers were wandering near where Ramapati was hiding in a trench. He surprised them with his gun pointed at them. They raised their hands to surrender. He forced them to lie on the ground. While he was tackling one of them the other tried to run away. He shot him dead. Then he used stranglehold to kill the other soldier, who was speaking German in pain as he couldn't breathe. Ramapati removed his foot from the German soldier's neck only after he died.

After Ramapati returned from the World War I, he got married. Unfortunately, his wife died, leaving three sons behind. Ramapati got married again. From this wife he also had three sons. The oldest, Sumant, ran away when he was twelve years old. He was not a good student as his school teachers complained to his father, and so Ramapati beat him often. Still Sumant was not improving. One day Ramapati tried the same stranglehold on Sumant. His screams were heard by his relatives next door but nobody came to his rescue. Sumant somehow managed to push aside Ramapati's foot from his neck and ran away. Ramapati's sons knew that their father used to beat not only Sumant but also his mother, Charu.

Sumant came home again when he was about eighteen years old. He saw Ramapati lying on a floor bed crying in pain from his serious arthritis. Ramapati asked him for water. Sumant gave him water and messaged his body with warm mustard oil.

Ramapati died after a few days, and all of his sons participated in his cremation on the bank of the Alaknanda River. All the sons shaved their heads, as is required after cremation, proof of their respect for their dead father! Charu, now a widow, knew how phony her stepsons were! She didn't observe any of the rituals for her husband or fast. She didn't like the belief that she would join her wife-beater husband in heaven after her death and meet his other wife with him in a heavenly abode. A place in heaven was not guaranteed, though. There are seven heavens and seven hells where dead people go according to their karma.

Actually, Charu felt relief. She was now free from her master (*malik*). Her good karma! Her master's death emboldened her. She became a little reformer, and her list of reforms was noteworthy.

1. If your husband beats you or any bully male threatens you, then cry for help rather than pray silently. Some villagers will hear your cries and come up to help you.
2. Do not slap your little children. They are defenseless. Their bodies are soft and tender. They don't understand what is good and what is bad.
3. If you have daughters only, don't call yourself childless. Don't hesitate to take help from your married daughters when you are too old to take care of yourself.
4. Teach your daughters to utter the names of their husbands and senior in-laws. Don't distort their names. Don't let them force you to use the Hindu custom of *ghunghat* (veil). Uttering their names or not observing the veil custom does not mean you are disrespectful.

5. Treat the 'untouchables' as equals. Share food and drink with them as you would with your family members.
6. Keep your village clean. Don't throw your filth in your streams. All streams here ultimately join the Ganges and pilgrims consider the Ganges' water as holy, bathe in it, and drink it, and even carry it home.
7. Guns are made to kill. Be careful.
8. Girls, like boys, must be sent to school. Goddesses like Sarasvati or Durga are unable to help female literacy. Building modern schools, not their temples, will.

These reforms come from her experiences, some very funny and some outrageous. For example, a woman in an adjacent village was ridiculed because she inadvertently uttered her husband's name as it was: Mohan. She insisted that she didn't say 'Mohan' but said 'Phohen' instead. She was ridiculed again and accused of saying 'Mohan' again.

In another adjacent village, some men were college educated, and one man there had daughters only. He performed a live funeral, or *jīvachhrāddha* (*jīvat-śrāddha*), ceremony at the town of Gaya on the banks of its river. After such a mock funeral, the performer does not need an actual funeral at his or her death. But that man had cousins who had sons who could have performed his real funeral. The Gaya priests are sure that such mock funerals guarantee heaven for the performer. Nevertheless, the priestly fees (*dakṣiṇā*) are guaranteed. Charu never thought that educated people would really go for such a stupid ritual -- one can die without dying! It's possible, only in India!

Charu, like all reformers, received some criticism and some praise. The only big Indian reformers she knew about were Swami Dayananda and Mahatama Gandhi. How Gandhi impacted the world was beyond her imagination. She was not educated enough to know that there have been reformers everywhere in the world as great as Gandhi, like Nelson Mandela and Dr. Martin Luther King, Jr. who suffered not from diseases but from bigotry, just like Gandhi.

Charu was very keen about sending girls to school, not just for basic literacy but for higher learning. Early marriage is devastating not only for these girls' lives but for the life of the entire country. More unwanted children, more financial burden. She has a vivid memory of a father who arranged his twelve-year-old daughter's marriage with a twenty-eight- year-old man. The girl ran away in the paddy fields and her father sent his son to catch her. She was forced to marry. Legally, a twelve-year-old girl's marriage was not allowed, but who cares about laws as long as the father gets good bride price!

Another case she knew of was as bad. A man, who was her relative, remained unmarried because of the foul game he faced. The girl's parents showed a girl to him. The girl was beautiful and he liked her, and so the marriage was fixed; but on the day of marriage some other girl sat on the marriage altar. That girl was the real daughter of those thug parents. Her relative had run away from the marriage altar.

Untouchability, Charu thought, has been a national crime for thousands of years. She remembered how a Brahmin woman of a nearby village was saved by an untouchable man. Due to heavy monsoon rains, the nearby forest stream became a raging river. The woman was out in the forest to herd cattle, and when the villagers looked for her, they found her standing helpless on the other side of the raging river. A man tried to help her cross the stream, but both were swept away. Luckily, a man downstream jumped into the current and brought both out safely. The woman didn't thank her savior because he was untouchable. That woman was observing a holy fast, which became polluted because she was in contact with an untouchable—and that was her only thought.

Some of Charu's critics had shallow national pride. Some were offended when she started a sort of slogan: Those cowards who created and supported untouchability must be rotting in hell. They didn't like her exposing the local problems to the world. She firmly believed that exposing problems, not hiding problems, was the right way to help the country. 'Someday things would change for good. And we will be proud' was her answer to the critics.

CHAPTER TWENTY-SIX

CHAITI CONTINUED TO reconstruct Bijli's family history as vividly as possible:

Ramapati's three sons from his first wife loved hunting. They all had rifles. The oldest son, Raghuvir, was college educated and became very friendly with the British administrator of Pauri, with whom he went into several adjacent forests to hunt. Raghuvir became a deputy collector, a very prestigious position, which allowed him to be a womanizer.

His wife was infected by his syphilis and was unable to cook. So, he hired a male cook who was from the lowest untouchable caste. His relatives didn't like it, but they did not dare to argue with him. After all, he was a deputy collector, respected as Collector Sahab.

On the day of his son Dhanu's birthday, he invited all the relatives. The cook prepared various dishes, and nobody objected that the food was cooked by an untouchable who occasionally ate the meat of a naturally dead buffalo, which was always avoided by the higher castes. Actually, they appreciated the *biranji*, a Garhwali word for biriyani. The Garhwali biranji was unique because it had a lot of goat intestine pieces, very tasty.

When Dhanu was studying biology at the University of Lucknow, he got the news that his father tried to rape a woman. It was also rumored that the deputy collector was secretly married to a woman in another village. The father and son stopped communicating, but the father kept sending Dhanu money.

One day Dhanu got the news that his mother died. He didn't know that the cause of her death was syphilis. He returned to his village and met his father, who insisted Dhanu visit the local Kali temple because his late mother was an ardent devotee of the goddess. Dhanu refused as he had found no existence of Kali or any goddess and gods in his biological studies. He didn't tell his father that he was in love with a classmate in Lucknow, Rangini, a Chandel Rajput girl. Dhanu didn't care for the stupid convention forbidding inter-caste marriage. After graduation, the two classmates got married in a court ceremony.

The following year the deputy collector, too, died of syphilis. Rangini insisted that Dhanu must go back to his village to perform the ritual of *śrāddha* (a memorial service) for his father. Dhanu and Rangini did go back and arrange the memorial. The old cook was happy to see the couple. Because the auji caste people who the cook belonged to are tailors and drummers, he asked his male relatives to play drums and bagpipes to welcome Dhanu and Rangini.

Then they shared sweets and various foods, including meatless biriyani, ignoring the tradition by which the upper castes and the untouchables were not allowed to eat together.

The cook told Rangini that her father in-law was a great hunter who killed deer, wild pig, wild pigeons, quail and other wild fowl. He showed her a room filled with the skins of tigers, deer, sheep, and bears.

"Sheep! Are there wild sheep nearby?"

"There are no wild sheep in our hills, but Collector Sahab liked mutton. He ate more food whenever I cooked mutton. He was also fond of collecting sheepskins. Some he spread on his bed to keep him warm during snowy winters."

Rangini looked dismayed as she believed in the conservation of wildlife. She did ask him if there were any lion skins because she had seen the pictures of Goddess Parvati riding a lion. The cook laughed. He knew that there were no lions in the Garhwal Himalayas. So, some ignorant artists showed Parvati riding a tiger, but he knew that any animal shown as a vehicle of a god or goddess was imaginary. He even joked with her that a mouse couldn't be a vehicle of such a bulky god like Lord Ganesh! Most Hindus would hate seeing any mice in their houses, but Lord Ganesha's vehicle is worshipped and praised in devotional songs, hoping that the Lord will remove any obstacle—but apparently not the obstacles of mice! Lord Ganesha's parents, Shiva and Parvati, were married in the Garhwal Himalayas. Nobody has seen them. People would have taken photos of Lord Ganesha riding his mouse, both talking to each other in Sanskrit!

Rangini smiled and looked amused by the cook's understanding of these deities.

The untouchable castes have their own supreme deity. That's *Nirankār*, which means Formless God. Ironically, local upper-caste Hindus respect *Nirankār* and consider the untouchables Hindus. Untouchables were not allowed to use Sanskrit or Vedic language. Not even today. The word *Nirankār*, however, is a Sanskrit derivative.

The cook didn't mention that a few untouchable leaders didn't consider them as Hindus, however. Some of them wanted to burn the holy book "Manu's Laws" (*Manusmṛti).* Some ridiculed the 'holy bath' in Ma Ganga. 'The untouchable is untouchable no matter how many times he takes a dip in the holy waters of the Ganges. Why did Ma Ganga fail to purify some of its own sinless children, the Shudras, since Vedic times?'

So, some of their fellow untouchables converted to Christianity and adopted English names, mostly Biblical, such as David, Joseph, Daniel, Jack, John, Moses, Solomon, Abraham, Rahel (Rachel), Mary, etc. They established their churches where they used Hindi rather than Sanskrit, so-called God's language, or *Deva vāṇī.* And they sang the Lord's prayer in Hindi. A very few converts knew that Jesus Christ spoke Aramaic, not the English of the King James

Bible, and they firmly believed that the Brahmins created the social partition of India in very ancient times—the Vedic *Varṇa* divisions of society and devastating caste discrimination were the proof. But these Christians, even though they were non-vegetarians, never believed in animal sacrifice; and their churches were open to anyone, including untouchables, unlike Hindu temples that were built by untouchables.

The cook praised the late deputy collector, who was happy to hire an untouchable cook. The cook told Rangini that some local fanatic Brahmins considered the cooked food touched by an untouchable very unhealthy. And if a Brahmin was eating food, an untouchable must not fix his gaze at that food because his gaze could make that food poisonous.

Rangini appeared shocked. The cook continued. Collector Sahab was different. The relatives of the cook were allowed to come into the kitchen and share food with Collector Sahab. In return, those relatives frequently offered their free services to the family of Collector Sahab. Some untouchable children began to go to school, and Collector Sahab gave them money to buy books and clothes and to pay tuition. Many educated Brahmins thought that the brains of untouchables were not fully developed. Collector Sahab never believed in such Brahmin thinking. He thought denying humanity to any people must be a crime.

"Finally, it did become a crime," the cook told her. Rangini nodded her head. 'Thanks to the new secular Indian Constitution and its framers, who abolished untouchability as a legal category. The framers' team included Brahmins, and the head of the team was an untouchable lawyer educated at the top universities of India, Great Britain, and the United States of America!'"

Tears began to flow from her beautiful eyes. The cook looked overwhelmed. He asked her, 'Why are you crying?'

She didn't respond and kept her eyes closed. The cook had no idea that she was dreaming of the first celebration of the new Constitution on the 26th of January, the Republic Day of India. Her

Christian high school's principal invited all the students to attend the celebration at noon. The students were surprised to have a free lunch, which was not an ordinary lunch but a grand feast. Rumali rotis, a round thin bread, outsizing the big plate on which it is served and dam alu, a special potato curry, with rewari sweets made with sesame seeds made this a memorable feast. Some students had fun with those giant-size round and thin *rumali rotis,* as foldable as napkins. How can such a large bread fit in a fist is a miracle of the Lucknow cuisine that started at the time of the Nawabs!

During the lunch, the principal gave a speech: "Boys and girls!" he said loudly while ringing a bell to get their attention. "This is the greatest day of our Indian history. Thanks to Mahatma Gandhi who, with his outstanding colleagues, made this day possible. Gandhi was a unique radical freedom fighter because he caused no harm to anyone. He taught us to continue our friendship with Great Britain and follow her democratic traditions. We will try to be a model democracy, not because India is now the largest democracy of the world but because we will treat the whole world as one family as promised in India's ancient saying, *Vasudhaiva kuṭumbakam.*"

Rangini felt especially honored when the principal came to her table and hugged her. "Rangini!" he said softly, "Now you and all the girls are equal with boys. I am wishing that gender equality is a reality as soon as possible for there is no real democracy without gender equality. Women will hold positions such as parliamentarians, governors, ambassadors, doctors, scientists, pilots, presidents, and prime ministers. Today our women wear sari, shalwar, lehanga, ghagri, kurta, kurti and blouses. Someday they will be brave soldiers wearing the same khaki military uniform as the men soldiers have. But some communities have gender-bias."

"I don't understand," Rangini said.

"That's because we don't have that kind of bias in the north. When a girl is married, the husband has the right to change her name. The girl has no such right. A wife is not owned by her husband. Her parents have raised their daughter with that name and later her husband disregards that name. The girl's parents have no voice. They simply accept this kind of male chauvinism."

Apparently, the principal was not aware of the fact that in the Garhwal hills, the northernmost part of India, a woman's husband is called her malik, her master. This northern tradition is a kind of women's slavery.

Thirteen-year-old Rangini laughed.

"What makes you laugh?" the principal asked.

"Sir, I don't think I will have any of the positions you just mentioned."

"You will if you want to. Just wait. You will see my prediction come true," the principal said in an authoritative tone. "Remember: If no veil for men, then no veil for women."

Rangini bowed, and with both hands she touched the feet of the principal to pay him the highest respect. The principal wiped his tears of joy as he placed his hand on her head to bless her.

When the feast was over, all stood up and sang the new national anthem of India: *Jana gana mana*. The anthem was not just an ordinary song; it was written by Rabindranath Tagore, the Nobel laureate of literature.

Then the principal surprised the students, announcing that there would be fireworks at the soccer field of the school that evening.

As the evening descended upon Lucknow, the amazing fireworks went up and up. The star-studded sky above seemed to be dazzled not only by the fireworks but also by the band music, consisting of trombones, recorders, flutes, trumpets, clarinets, and Western drums. All the musicians were dressed in white jackets and pants below their red hats. They were led by a small group of male dancers dressed in the same attire as the musicians.

At the corner of the soccer field was a stage where the principal's teenager son and daughter were seated, holding the tricolor Indian flag in their hands.

Suddenly, those attending heard the sounds of anklets (*ghunghrus*) worn by the barefooted female dancers. A team of dancers appeared on the stage and bowed to the audience with the Lucknow-style *salam* greetings. Then they started their Katthak Dance, which was developed during the Nawab rule of Lucknow. The music was fascinating, and the young female dancers wore colorful dresses of the Nawab times. The male musicians wore the *sherwani* (an Indian topcoat) and the tight white pajamas. The male coach of the team was uttering the *bols*, the musical words, for the dancers and drummers to mimic with their anklets and tablas. The harmonium player used the morning *raga bhairavi* to symbolize the morning of Indian democracy.

A few men were so impressed by the whole performance that they too began to dance, moving in a frenzy toward the stage. Then in appreciation of the musicians, they put rupee notes in front of the drummers and the harmonium player.

GLOSSARY

Achhut: untouchable, lowest caste people (*achhūt*)

Aheri: female ghost (*aheṛi*)

Ahimsa, ahinsa: Sanskrit *ahiṃsā*, non-killing, non-violence

Akhara: a religious circle

Aligarh: a city in North India

Allahabad: a city in North India (lit. God's City). Its older name is *Prayag* "Confluence" as it is situated at the confluence of the Ganges and Yamuna rivers.

Arti: worship ritual with ghee-soaked lighted cotton wicks

Athwar: a sacrifice (*aṭhwaṛ*) in which a male buffalo is beaten to death (Sanskrit *aṣṭavāra* "the *eighth day* of goddess worship")

Auji: a lower caste, comprised of drummers and tailors

Avatar: incarnation of God

Ayodhya: a holy city in North India, Lord Rama's capital

Baba: father, or holy man

Badrinath: a holy town in the Garhwal Himalayas with a Vishnu temple

Bahin: sister

Basmati: a long-grained fragrant rice

Basudhara Falls: the waterfall near Badrinath in the Garhwal Himalayas

Bhabhi: sister-in-law, elder brother's wife

Bhagwan, Bhagawan: God (Sanskrit *Bhagavān*)

Bhagavad Gita: an ancient philosophical discourse in Sanskrit between Krishna and Arjuna

Bhagavata Purana: an ancient sacred book in Sanskrit (*Bhāgavata Purāṇa*)

Bhagawati: Bhagavati (*Bhagavatī*), Goddess

Bhagiratha: a king (an ancestor of King Rama of Ayodhya)

Bhai: brother

Bhairavi: a morning *raga* of Indian classical music, named after Goddess Parvati.

Bhajan: devotional song

Bhangra: the popular folk dance form of Punjab, India

Bharata: King Bharata whose parents were Dushyanta and Shakuntala. India is named after him as Bharat (*Bhārata*).

Bhikkhu: monk (Buddhist)

Bhikkhuni: nun (Buddhist)

Bhikshu: monk, male beggar

Bhikshuni: nun, female beggar

Bhot: a word for Tibet

Bhotant: another name for Tibet, used in the Garhwal Himalayas

Bhotia: a person belonging to an Indian-Tibetan community of the Garhwal Himalayas

Bhut: male ghost (*bhūt*)

Bijli: lightning, a name for girls

Biriyani, biryani: a spicy fried rice dish

Bols: the rhythmic words to be mimicked by the drums and anklets

Brahma: God of creation, created by Lord Vishnu

Brahmin: the highest social class in Hinduism, priestly caste

But-Parast: Buddha-followers. The Urdu word for idol-worshippers, derived from Farsi.

Chana: chickpeas

Char Dham: the four holy places (Badrinath, Kedarnath, Gangotri, Yamunotri) in the Garhwal Himalayas

Chhole: a spicy dish made with chickpeas

Dalit: a low caste person (same as achhūt or ḍom)

Damau: a timpani-shaped drum

Dam alu: a potato curry

Dangchaura: a village in the Garhwal Himalayas

Darshan: to view, or seeing a deity

Dasharatha: King Rama's father

Deva Bhumi: God's land (the Indian state of Uttarakhand is frequently called the "God's land" or the land of gods)

Devanagari: the script used for Sanskrit, Hindi etc.

Dhol: a bass drum *ḍhol*

Doli: a carriage for the bride, used to carry her away to her husband's home

Dom, doma: untouchable person called *ḍom* or *ḍūm*

Dumana: the segregated colony or living section of the untouchables called *ḍumaṇā*

Durga: a goddess

Dushyanta: the king who was husband of Shakuntala and father of King Bharata after whose name India is called Bharat.

Four Holy Places: (See Char Dham)

Ganga: the Ganges river

Gangotri: a holy town on the banks of the Ganges in the Garhwal Himalayas

Garhwal: a Central Himalayan region of the Uttarakhand state of India

Garhwal Himalayas: a region of the Central Himalayas

Garhwali: an Indo-Aryan language of the Garhwal Himalayas

Gauri: a name of the goddess Parvati (Sanskrit *Gaurī* "White")

Ghar jamain: a man who lives with his in-laws after marriage

Ghee: clarified butter

Ghunghat, ghungat: veil

Gita-Govinda: Gītagovinda, Song of God (a poetic work in Sanskrit authored by Jayadeva)

Gomukh: The place in the Garhwal Himalayas from where the Ganges starts.

Gomutra: *gomūtra* "cow urine"

Gopi: a cowgirl, Lord Krishna's friend

Gori: a white woman

Gurudwara: a temple of the Sikhs

Gurukul, Gurukula: lit. Guru's School; ancient educational schools in India

Hanumān Chālīsā: a booklet of forty couplets authored by the poet Tulsidas

Har, Hara: God, one of the names of Lord Shiva

Har ki Pairi: a sacred spot on the banks of the Ganges in Haridwar

Har Mandir Sahib: Golden Temple of the Sikhs situated in Amritsar, a holy city in the Indian state of Punjab

Haridwar, Hardwar: a holy Himalayan town, situated on the banks of the Ganges

Hausa: A Nigerian language

Havan: fire worship with ghee-mixed oblations

Himanchal: the Himalayas

Hindi: an official language of India

Hindutva: Hinduism

Hittite: an ancient Anatolian language belonging to the Indo-European family of languages

Hopi: an American Indian language of Arizona

Hottentot: a South African language

Hymn of Man: the *Puruṣa Sūkta* from the *Rigveda*, which divides the society into four classes: Brahmins, Kshatriyas, Vaishyas, and Shudras

Id or Eid: a Muslim festival

I.A.S.: Indian Administrative Service; an officer of this service

Jogini: a female *yogi*; nun

Joshimath: a holy town in the Garhwal Himalayas

Kabuli: belonging to Kabul

Kandi: a village in Garhwal

Kandyal: a native of the village Kandi

Kaṇva: a sage who had adopted Shakuntala as his daughter, wife of King Dushyanta and mother of King Bharata

Kaṛi: a type of curry made with yogurt

Karnaprayag: a holy town in the Garhwal Himalayas

Kashmir: a Western Himalayan region divided between India and Pakistan

Katthak: a dance form developed in Lucknow during the Nawab times

Kedarnath: Lord Shiva's name; a Shiva temple in the Garhwal Himalayas

Kerala: the southern coastal state of India

Khavas: a term used for the concubines of the Tehri Maharaja of the Garhwal Himalayas

Kravi: meat

Krishna: an incarnation of Lord Vishnu

Kshatriya: the warrior class in the *varṇa* system of India

Kulcha: a spicy fried bread

Kumbh Mela: the holy Pot Fair

Kurta: a man's tunic shirt with no collar

Kurti: a woman's tunic shirt with no collar

Lakshmi: the wife of Lord Vishnu and goddess of wealth

Lila, Līlā: play, game, sport

Linga: symbolizing Lord Shiva's phallus

Lucknow: a city in northern India, and the capital of the state of Uttar Pradesh

Ma: mother

Madhyamaheshwar: a holy place in the Garhwal Himalayas, one of the abodes of Lord Shiva

Mahabharata, Mahābhārata: an ancient epic in Sanskrit

Mahant: the head priest of a temple

Maharaja: a Hindu king; lit. great king

Mahishasuramardini: a name of the goddess Parvati (Sanskrit *Mahiṣāsuramardinī* "Buffalo-Demon-Beater")

Malik: master, owner (used also for a husband in Garhwali).

Malkauns: a raga of Indian classical music

Mana: an Indian village situated in the Garhwal Himalayas near the Tibet border

Mandakini: a tributary of the Alakananda river flowing through the Garhwal Himalayas

Mandir: temple

Manusmriti: the book *Manusmṛti* "Laws of Manu."

Mathura: a holy city in North India, situated on the banks of the Yamuna river

Mausi: mother's sister

Meghanāda: a son of Rāvaṇa

Moksha: *Mokṣa*, salvation; liberation from rebirth

Moradabad: a town in North India

Mṛgayā, Mrigayā: hunting

Mṛtyu: death; mortality

Mullah: a Muslim priest

Mumbai: a city in India, formerly known as Bombay

Naga sadhu: a naked saint (*Nāga*)

Namaste: a greeting; lit. "Bow to you"

Nambudiri: a Brahmin caste of the Kerala state of India

Namli: a girl born who can marry only a boy born under the same constellation under which she was born

Nawab: a Muslim king

Nirvana: *Nirvāṇa,* salvation; freedom from rebirth; lit. non-breath or breathless hence death

Pakora: spicy fritters

Pandit or Pundit: a Brahmin priest

Panjabi, Punjabi: a person from the Punjab region divided between India and Pakistan; the language spoken in Punjab

Paramatma: *Paramātmā* "Supreme Self, God"

Prana: *prāṇa* "breath, breathing, life"

Prana-pratishtha: *prāṇa-pratiṣṭhā* "life-establishment." Used to consider a sacred icon a live deity.

Pranam: *praṇāma* "special bow." A salutation word used with folded hands while optionally touching the feet of a respected person.

Puja. *Pūjā* "Worship"

Pyasa: *Pyāsā* "thirsty"

Rajasthan: an Indian state

Rama, Rāma: the king of Ayodhya and the hero of the epic Ramayana

Ramayana, Rāmāyaṇa: an ancient epic in Sanskrit

Rampur: a city in northern India named after Lord Rama

Randi: a prostitute

Rasgulla: a type of Indian dessert

Raval: *Rāval* "the head priest"

Riddhi: one of the wives of Lord Ganesha

Rigveda: the first Vedic scripture

Rishi: a sage; seer

Rudraprayag: a holy town in the Garhwal Himalayas and the confluence of the rivers Alakananda and Mandakini

Rumali roti: a big, thin, round flat bread

Sahab: an honorific term to address a man (same as sahib)

Sahib: (See sahab)

Salam, Salām: a greeting, salutation

Sanatana Dharma, Sanātana Dharma: eternal religion, an ancient name of Hinduism

Sarasvati, Sarasvatī: Hindu Goddess of learning and speech

Sardar: a respectful word for a Sikh man; lit. chief

Shah: a king

Shaivite: belonging to Lord Shiva

Shalwar, salwar: loose pants or pajamas

Shaivite: belonging to Lord Shiva, a part of Hinduism

Sherwani: Indian-style topcoat for men

Shia: a part of Islam

Shiva: Lord Shiva (lit. good)

Shudra, śūdra: the lowest Hindu social class; untouchable

Siddhi: one of the wives of Lord Ganesha, success

Sikh: a follower of Sikhism founded by Guru Nanak

Sikhism: a religion founded by Guru Nanak

Srinagar: a city in the Garhwal Himalayas, situated on the banks of Alakananda

Sufi, Sūfī: a sect of the Muslim religion

Sunni: a part of Islam

Talaq, talāq: divorce

Tanga, Tāngā: a horse carriage

Tangawala, Tāngāwālā: driver of a horse carriage or *tāngā*

Tehri: a town in the Garhwal Himalayas, situated on the banks of the Ganges

Three Jewels: the three vows, known as Tri-ratnas, to convert to Buddhism: I take refuge in the Buddha; I take refuge in the Dharma; I take refuge in the Sangha (the Buddhist Order).

Tulsidas. Tulasīdāsa: a Moghul Brahmin poet who wrote the epic *Rāmacharitamānasa* in the Avadhi language. He considered King Rama of the ancient Sanskrit epic *Rāmāyaṇa* as an avatar of God.

U.P.: Uttar Pradesh, a northern state of India

Uttar Pradesh: same as U.P.

Vaishnavite: belonging to Lord Vishnu (*Viṣṇu*), a part of Hinduism

Varanasi: the holy city of Banaras (Benaras) in northern India, situated on the banks of the Ganges

Varna: the Hindu social class system of *Varṇa*; lit. "variation" based on profession and color

Vasudhaiva kuṭumbakam: "The world alone is the family"

Veda: the oldest Hindu scriptures; knowledge

Vedika: the Vedic altar (*Vedikā*)

Vidushaka: *Vidūṣaka* "court jester."

Vishnu, *Viṣṇu*: the Vedic god who has many non-Vedic avatars, including Lord Rama, Lord Krishna, and other Puranic avatars such as Nara-Siṃha (half man-half lion)

Vrata: vow

Yajurveda: one of the four *Vedas*: The other three are *Rigveda, Sāmaveda, and Atharvaveda.* These are the earliest scriptures.

ABOUT THE AUTHOR

ANOOP CHANDOLA IS an Indian American linguist-anthropologist (a U.S. citizen). He was born in an Uttarakhand Himalayan Brahmin family of India and inherited priestly profession. Though his father broke his ancestral polygamous tradition the family suffered the aftereffects of polygamy. He was educated at the universities of Allahabad and Lucknow. His last two degrees in linguistics include an M.A. from the University of California, Berkeley, and a Ph.D. from the University of Chicago. He has taught Indian literature, culture, and religion at several universities in India and the U.S.A., including Sardar Patel University, the M.S. University of Baroda, the University of California at Berkeley, the University of Washington at Seattle, the University of Texas at Austin, and the University of Wisconsin at Madison. He retired from the University of Arizona as Professor Emeritus of East Asian Studies. He has been a member of numerous professional associations, including the American Anthropological Association, the Association for Asian Studies, the Linguistic Society of America, and the Linguistic Society of India. Chandola has published numerous papers and sixteen books including four novels. His scholarly research covers linguistics, music, religion, and literature, including extensive interdisciplinary and theoretical analysis. He lives with his wife Sudha in Tucson and Kent, near Seattle. More details about him are available on Wikipedia. He can be contacted by his email: anoopchandola@gmail.com

Printed in the United States
by Baker & Taylor Publisher Services